HAND ME THE REINS

BACHELOR AUCTION - 3

VANESSA VALE

Hand Me The Reins by Vanessa Vale

Copyright © 2021 by Bridger Media

Cover design: Bridger Media

Cover graphic: Wander Aguiar Photography; Deposit Photos: design west

GET A FREE VANESSA VALE BOOK!

Join Vanessa's mailing list to be the first to know of new releases, free books, special prices and other author giveaways.

http://freeromanceread.com

HATCHER

FRIDAY NIGHT

I WAS the last single man standing. All the others had been sold off like bulls at the county fair. Bought by the highest bidding woman, who most likely wanted a wild ride with a prime stud. I was sure that wasn't what Reverend Abernathy had in mind as he MC'd the charity bachelor auction. A coffee date. Maybe lunch or a summer evening ice cream cone.

Alice, our family housekeeper and the woman who'd volunteered me and my brothers for the event, probably agreed. But she wanted us paired off and knew it wasn't going to happen playing Scrabble. Maybe naked Twister. Now that could be fun.

"Last but not least," Reverend Abernathy said, clapping his hands once, joining me backstage. "This has turned out to be a bigger success than we ever imagined."

The glee on his face at the sum being raised to help the youth program at the community center couldn't be missed.

"I'm glad it's working out," I replied.

"You can do it again next year," he encouraged.

Next year? Hell, no. I'd been debating an offer to run a bar in Cozumel for the winter while my buddy Kent went on a once in a lifetime trek across Africa. Kent had called a few weeks ago, giving me time to consider. I had the job qualifications. Besides needing a lot of sunscreen and buying a pair of swim trunks, I could easily take over. But the reverend's suggestion of me being in another bachelor auction had me in Mexico before the first frost and maybe staying longer than just the winter.

I hadn't made a final decision yet, but the man of God sure was helping.

He tapped his lip with a finger. "I have a feeling the pool of eligible bachelors may be a little smaller."

"You mean Huck and Sarah." My brother and Sarah O'Banyon had been sweethearts years ago, but they'd broken up. Hadn't talked since. Until just now when Sarah had bought Huck in the auction. I had no idea why she'd done it, but she'd put in the only bid, and a high one, so she had a reason.

He shrugged. "There is hope they will have their happy ending."

I hoped I could have a happy ending with my date, and not the permanent kind. A quickie that left us both sweaty and satisfied was just fine with me.

With that eager thought in mind, I set my hand on the reverend's shoulder and gave him my patented smile. "Let's do this."

He nodded and led me out onto the stage, then picked up the microphone to be heard over the rowdy group of women. I gave a little wave and they clapped.

"Last up is Thatcher Manning. Let's see if he can top his brothers' high bids."

"Ten dollars," a woman from the back shouted.

Everyone laughed at the small amount and I offered a small bow.

The bidding slowly rose and I recognized a few of the women who'd called out.

"Seventy-five dollars."

Everyone looked to the latest bidder who was at one of the round tables in the center of the room. Miss Turnbuckle. The elderly town librarian. Gray hair pulled back in a bun. White blouse beneath a pale blue cardigan. Reading glasses dangling by a chain.

Sawyer, Huck, and I had joked earlier in the week that she'd probably bid on one of us.

And she had. Me.

Inwardly, I sighed. There was going to be coffee. Idle chatting, although Miss Turnbuckle and I both had a love of reading and we could discuss books. *Books*. No happy ending, that was for fucking sure.

I felt a twinge of disappointment. Sawyer had carried a redhead over his shoulder, fireman style, from the auditorium. Huck had been bought by an old flame.

"Any other bids?" the reverend called.

No one spoke up. Only whispers and murmurs could be heard.

Of course no one was going to now. Who would ruin the older woman's chance? I didn't know if Miss Turnbuckle had bid on any of the other guys, but it seemed she'd let the other women have their turn at winning a bachelor. Now it was hers.

Me.

Actually, this was good. Fine. I didn't need any kind of clingy woman thinking that buying me at a bachelor auction was going to be more than a *date*. I didn't do attachments. Girlfriends. Long term.

A night of sweaty, energetic sex was one thing, but a relationship? Not a chance.

That wasn't going to happen with Miss Turnbuckle.

The date would be simple. I'd pick her up at her

door, take her for coffee, behave like the perfect
gentleman and talk about the latest mystery bestseller
and deliver her safely and happily back home.

I'd still give her a sly smile at the library whenever I
went in, but she wouldn't read into it or make
assumptions.

"Going once."

I could do this. A few hours and my good deed for
the kids of The Bend would be done. I winked at the
librarian, who narrowed her eyes seeing right through
my charm. As usual.

"Twice... sold!" Reverend Abernathy called.
"Thank you all for coming and supporting the youth
center. For those who have upcoming dates with this
fine group of bachelors, have fun."

The ladies clapped at the reverend's closing
remarks.

I nodded to him and made my way to Miss Turnbuckle. It took some time to cut through the crowd
now that the event was over.

The seat beside her was open and I settled into it,
taking off my hat. "Looking forward to our date, but
remember, I'm an impressionable young man, Miss T. I
need to be home by ten or Alice will ground me."

She tipped her head back and laughed. I always
liked the woman. I'd actually enjoyed going to the
library with my mother when I was little. Still did.
Unlike Sawyer and Huck, I liked to read and spent the

long winters in the overstuffed chair by my fireplace with a good book. Miss Turnbuckle often set aside something she thought I would enjoy, and she was usually right.

"No doubt." She looked up at a someone who passed and gave her a wave, then returned her attention to me.

"If I were fifty years younger, Thatcher Manning," she began, reaching out to give my hand a pat. "We'd go to Lake Delta and do some things that would frighten the fish."

I felt my cheeks heat as I ran a hand over the back of my neck.

"Don't scare him, Aunt Jean." A woman came around behind me, leaned down and kissed Miss Turnbuckle on the cheek. My gaze ran over her. Average height. Brown hair that was pulled back into a thick braid down her back. She had on jeans and a white and blue striped shirt. While the outfit was far from memorable, I couldn't miss the way the horizontal lines accentuated the full swells of her breasts.

And I was a breast man, for fucking sure. I guessed hers were more than a handful. Two lush mounds to get lost between.

She settled into the seat on the other side of her aunt and pushed a pair of thick glasses up her nose. I hadn't known Miss Turnbuckle had any relatives. As I thought about it, I had no idea where she lived. In fact, I just assumed she lived at the library.

"He's thirty years old. He should be past frightening," Miss Turnbuckle countered.

How she knew my exact age, I'd never know. Another one of the things she filed away in that brain of hers.

"I'm sorry I'm late," she said, offering me, then her aunt a smile. "God, I *hate* being late, but the Pardue wedding was relocated at the last minute and no one told me. I barely got the cake there in time."

"This is my great-niece, Astrid," Miss Turnbuckle said, then tipped her head toward me. "Astrid, Thatcher Manning. I hooked him into reading with the *Hardy Boys* series when he was seven and has been reading mysteries ever since."

I scratched the back of my neck. I was usually known as one of the infamous Manning brothers or the guy who owned the Lucky Spur. Or both. A lover, definitely, but not a *book* lover.

I shifted my gaze back to Astrid. She darted a glance my way. I couldn't see a hint of makeup on her face, although there was something white on her flushed cheek.

"Hey there," I said. I'd have tipped my hat, but it was on the table.

"Hi," she offered, although her gaze was focused on

my chin before she turned her attention to her aunt once again. "I can't believe you went through with it."

Miss Turnbuckle patted her hand. "Thatcher will do exactly what you want."

My eyebrows went up, unsure of what *exactly* Astrid wanted. When Astrid glanced at me with a hint of panic, I was definitely intrigued.

"Astrid owns the Flour Power bakery on South Chester," Miss Turnbuckle informed, which explained the smudge on Astrid's cheek.

Astrid was what I'd call a curvy girl, one who might like to eat delicious treats besides just making them. I liked that. A lot. A guy—or at least me—wanted something to grab onto when he fucked, dips and swells to get to touch and kiss and explore.

Fuck, what a way to go.

I wasn't sure if she was shy or if I scared her. Huck was definitely the scary Manning brother. I was the easygoing one, so for Astrid, I assumed shy.

"I'm sorry that I've never been to your shop before," I told her, making small talk. "I believe Alice bought a strawberry shortcake earlier in the summer."

There went the flush on her cheeks again. She looked at me, head on, for the first time. Her eyes, behind her glasses, were the greenest I'd ever seen. Like emeralds.

I felt like I was in a cartoon where a huge anvil fell on my head. My dick went instantly hard, and I was suddenly pleased she was shy because I wanted what- ever she was hiding behind those glasses and modest outfit. I had the insane desire to poke any guy's eyes out if he noticed her, too.

"Yes, that is a customer favorite during strawberry season," she replied. "I think it's the whipped cream since I put Kirsh in it."

Her voice was soft and gentle but somehow, I only thought of dark and dirty things that could be done with *whipped cream.* I wanted to do them with her. She wasn't coming on to me like women did at the Lucky Spur. Hell, she wasn't even trying, only talking with enthusiasm as someone who enjoyed her work.

Still, I had to shift in my chair at the surprised hit of arousal wondering if I licked the sweet confection off her nipples if they would be the color—and taste— of strawberries.

Yeah, I was single-minded.

What exactly did Astrid the baker *want* from me? Orgasms? Not a problem, especially if she brought her shortcake on the date.

Miss Turnbuckle pushed back her chair and stood. I hopped to my feet. My parents might have died when I was twelve, but they'd drilled into me good manners early on. Alice had finished that job with a wooden spoon a time or two.

I turned slightly and folded my hands together in front of me to hopefully hide the semi I was now sporting. Because of a shy baker. In front of the octogenarian librarian.

What the fuck was wrong with me?

"It's time for me to take my old bones home to bed," Miss Turnbuckle said. "I've got three more chapters in my book I'm eager to get to. If it ends like I think, I'll save it for you to check out."

"Don't we need to plan when I'll pick you up?" I asked.

She shook her head, patted my arm, then squeezed the muscle, her white eyebrows winging up. "I might have bought you, but the date's with Astrid."

Miss Turnbuckle waved to someone behind me and headed off in that direction.

My date was with *Astrid?* This bachelor auction was looking better and better by the minute. I turned my attention to the subtle beauty before me. Astrid looked up with those big green eyes.

"I need a man," she said, then slapped a hand over her mouth.

The four words were followed by a flush so bright I had to wonder if her pussy was that color after a hard fuck.

I bit back a groan at the thought.

This... whatever this was with Astrid, it was happening. If Astrid needed a man, I sure as shit was going to be it. And she'd get her money's worth.

 STRID

I NEED A MAN?

What the hell was wrong with me? I just told Thatcher Manning—*Thatcher Manning*—that I needed a man. If aliens could beam me up at this moment, I'd gladly go.

He must think I was insane. No, I *was* insane for blurting that.

I had to fix this... and fast. Instead of running away screaming, Thatcher offered some kind of weird huff of a laugh and dropped into Aunt Jean's now empty seat. His knee bumped mine beneath the table.

I glanced at him... barely, then away, then back.

"God, I sound creepy and desperate," I admitted. "Can we forget any of this ever happened?"

He slowly shook his head and I had to take in his ginger hair. It appeared to be recently cut, the sides trimmed short, the top a touch longer, natural curl making it look a bit unruly. Then I focused on his pale eyes that were lit with humor and curiosity, not fear of a crazy woman.

"Not a chance. I definitely want to know why you need a man." He put emphasis on the word *definitely.*

"I need a date. To my sister's wedding," I admitted. Going alone was bad enough I'd brought up the idea to Aunt Jean of buying a date at the auction to go with me. Which she'd taken to heart and done just that.

Bought me a bachelor. A good one, too. Thatcher Manning was *all* man. Six feet plus of muscled perfection. I'd never heard one bad thing about him—and gossip made its way into the bakery. And he was gorgeous. This close I could see the auburn stubble on his jaw. The way his full lips tipped up in amusement. The slight crook to his nose reminding me that while I thought he was perfect, he might not be after all. I wasn't looking for perfection. Hell, I wasn't even looking, but a fake date as hot as him? Worked for me.

Except I hated needing help. Growing up, whenever I asked for it, I got more of a lecture on doing things wrong than anything else, so I'd given up. Took care of myself. When I moved to The Bend, I'd decided to open Flour Power. My family—except for Aunt Jean —hadn't thought a bakery was a good business idea and figured I'd fail. I'd done it on my own and with tons of hard work, it was doing well. Going solo worked for me. Except in this one instance.

"Why didn't you bid on me, sweets?" he asked.

"Sweets?" I practically squeaked. I wasn't a total dork, but I definitely wasn't used to having a guy like Thatcher's attentions *very* focused on me. I wasn't a total dud when it came to guys and dating, but no one in the past—or most likely in the future—would melt my butter like he did.

And I knew *a lot* about butter.

Sitting this close, his voice was softer, although the deep rasp still raked over every nerve. As in every nerve in my nipples. They were hard points and I had to hope weren't noticeable through my top.

He leaned in. I held my breath because... Thatcher. Manning. Was. Breathing. Me. In.

"You smell like vanilla."

"A... a work thing," I whispered, tilting my head to the side because his nose was hovering right above my neck. So of course I rambled. "I just delivered a wedding cake."

"Mmm," he murmured and I felt that in my clit. "I bet you taste just as good as that cake."

"I... I—" What the heck did one say to that? Because all I could think about was *where* he wanted to taste me. My pussy clenched as I envisioned seeing his red hair between my thighs.

"Why didn't you bid on me?" he asked again.

I blinked, realized I'd let my eyes fall closed as I conjured up very dirty thoughts about him. "Because no one would outbid Aunt Jean."

Thatcher moved away, then laughed. "You're right. Smart thinking."

When he reached in and rubbed my cheek with his thumb, I sucked in a breath.

"Flour?" he asked.

The realization I'd been sitting here with flour on my face had me blushing and I pushed my glasses up out of habit. It was a reality check because there was no way Thatcher was going to go down on me in anything but my fantasies. "Oh, um... thanks. Job hazard."

"It's better than spilled beer," he replied, his gaze roving over my face as if... memorizing it?

"That's right. You own the Lucky Spur. I've only been there a few times. For lunch," I admitted. "I work all the time and am in bed early because I have to be up to bake at four."

"On the weekends, that's when I go to sleep," he admitted. "So, a date to your sister's wedding?"

The auditorium was emptying quickly now. Only a few people remained chatting.

Right. He was a bought date. Nothing more. Which

was exactly the point. A string-free, emotionless business arrangement. But as I looked at Thatcher, I realized that might be hard to do. Why had Aunt Jean chosen him specifically? Why not Graham Armstrong with whom I had zero connection?

I nodded, remembering he'd asked a question. "Next Sunday. I'm not in the wedding party so it won't be too bad for you. Like being caught in wedding pictures or a receiving line."

"Your sister's getting married and you're not a bridesmaid?"

I glanced away, moved an empty glass that had been left on the table. "Oh, no. I don't fit into the dress she picked out for them."

He frowned, then looked me over. I tried not to squirm as he did so. I wasn't a supermodel. Hell, it was more like I'd eaten a supermodel. I was short and curvy. *Very* curvy. Boobs and hips and ass. I'd won the trifecta of *big* body parts, unlike my sister, Amy. And my mother, the former Miss Western Montana.

"What the hell does that even mean?" he asked.

I waved off his question because really, what woman wanted to have to say out loud that her family thought she was fat? That she had a job that kept her that way?

Neither of it was true. I'd been... *big boned* all my life. Exercise wasn't going to make my boobs any smaller or make me grow six inches taller.

I was content in my body, except where my family was concerned.

"Don't worry, I'm not looking for a relationship or anything," I added quickly. "That's why I thought this auction thing would work. I don't want you to get the wrong idea, that I'm desperate or clingy. This way—"

"I'm paid for my services," he finished for me.

My mouth fell open and my heart began a double-time beat realizing I may have offended him. "I'd never—"

He laughed. "I'm messing with you." Leaning in again, he looked left and right as if to ensure no one was nearby. "But if you were seeking *additional* services, I can deliver those too. On the house."

I stared. And stared. And then blinked.

A slow smile spread across his face. "Your aunt didn't have to buy me."

"We talked about it," I told him. "What I was going to do about the wedding. The fact that I wanted to bring someone. When I first heard about the bachelor auction, I thought buying a date would solve my problems. I'd been joking. Sort of. I didn't think Aunt Jean was actually going to bid, although I should have known."

Everyone underestimated Aunt Jean. Being the town librarian since the dawn of time, she was considered an old maid, a virgin with delicate sensibilities. If they only knew. She made *me* look like that. I wasn't a virgin, but it had been so long, and not very good, that I might as well be.

"Like I said, you didn't have to buy a date with me. You could have come by the bar and asked. I'd have said yes."

Now it was my turn to laugh. "There's no way I could have asked you out. Ever."

He cocked his head. "Why not? I'm not that bad, am I?"

Him? Bad? I studied him, perhaps a little too thoroughly, because I realized I'd been doing it for a long number of seconds. So of course, I flushed. Again. I licked my dry lips. "No. Not bad at all."

Perhaps almost too good to be believable. My family would wonder how someone like me could snag a guy like Thatcher.

He leaned in. It seemed to be something he did, giving someone his complete attention and focus. "It's really important that you take a date, isn't it?"

"You have no idea," I countered, impossible to keep the bitterness from my voice.

"Why?"

"Because my ex is going to be there," I grumbled. I'd known this for months and it still sucked. "He's... the best man."

He winced, as if in sympathy. "Shit. I can see how that would make for a miserable time. You're not over him?"

I huffed and crossed my arms. "Oh, I'm *very* over him. But... well, you'll see next Sunday, if you say yes."

I practically held my breath as I waited for him to give me his answer.

He nodded once. "Done. Next Sunday, I'll be the best bought date you ever had."

I was elated, and a little freaked because what if he was right? What if a guy my aunt bought for me at a charity bachelor auction really was the best date I ever had?

3

 STRID

"YES, Mother. I will have the cake done on time."

I had my cell squeezed between my shoulder and my ear as I changed piping nozzles, then began to add a border of buttercream to the top tier of the cake I was finishing. Mary, the woman who worked for me part time, came into the kitchen and rolled her eyes at my half of the conversation. She'd been working for me for a year and knew my family well. Knew *of* them since they'd never once come into the bakery. They didn't come to The Bend, preferring to stay in their little rich and crazy bubble in Cutthroat.

"Do you think you can create the flowers we talked about?" she asked. "I emailed you a photo of them."

"I got the—"

I heard fumbling, then my sister. "It's crucial they match the bridal bouquet."

Taking a deep breath, I paused in my piping, not wanting my frustration at Bridezilla to mess up my work. "I know, Amy. You've told me several times."

I couldn't miss the huff. "Well, I just want it to be perfect."

I put the piping bag down on the worktable, grabbed my cell so I didn't get a crick in my neck. "It *will* be perfect," I countered. My work was *never* less than that. I had pride in my business, in the products I delivered.

My older sister was exceptional at passive aggressiveness. I hadn't gone to her offering my services to make a four-tiered lemon poppyseed wedding cake. She and my mother had chosen me. Because I'd do it for free most likely. My parents and sister were rich enough to host a two-hundred-person wedding, but cheap enough to nickel and dime their own family member, then question her abilities.

"Looking forward to seeing it on Friday," she replied.

I stilled. "Friday? I was going to bring it Saturday afternoon before the rehearsal dinner."

"I want to see it before the bachelorette party so there's time in case you have to fix it."

Gritting my teeth, I glanced at Mary. "What bachelorette party?" I asked Amy.

Mary rolled her eyes.

"I didn't tell you about it?"

No, she hadn't told me about it, which meant she had never intended to invite me. We weren't close, never had been. Her friends had been just that, hers. But I was her sister and at a minimum, she should have figured people would question her as to why I wasn't there. What other people thought—besides me—was important to her.

There was a pause. "It's Friday night. My wedding planner should have contacted you."

"Why would *she* tell me about *your* party?"

"Because I'm so busy, silly. Bring the cake Friday at seven to the hotel."

As if I wasn't busy. My *little business* as Amy and Mother called it was booming. The Bend liked their treats and I had steady customers. The addition last summer of the coffee bar meant I had people stopping in all morning long to visit with friends or grab and go a pick-me-up. I glanced at the calendar on the wall filled in with all the special orders and events already booked. Besides

Amy's cake, I had two others to complete for the following weekend. Another wedding cake and one for a baby shower.

I had my schedule planned out far in advance and shifting Amy's cake up a day affected all my work. Even my supplies.

"And you can try on your dress. We need time to plan accordingly."

"Accordingly for what?" While I wasn't in the wedding, my mother had picked out a dress for me to wear. I'd been doubly hurt at first, but I'd had months to get over the fact that I wasn't pretty enough to be a bridesmaid or that they thought I wouldn't select something appropriate.

As Aunt Jean had said, it was better this way. Out of sight, out of mind. I hadn't had to worry about a dress nor the implications my choice would bring.

"To make sure the dress fits. You know how you put on those pounds. Running a bakery isn't good for someone like you."

I didn't *put on pounds*. My weight had stayed the same since eleventh grade. I'd been a late bloomer, but I'd definitely bloomed. A lot. Hips. Boobs. Lots of curves. I wasn't skinny like Amy.

"But it's okay for someone like you to have a sister who's a baker because then you get a free cake?" I snapped.

She was silent for a moment. "Why do you have to

be so petty? Is this about Edward? Your inability to keep him shouldn't be taken out on me."

I rubbed my temple because a headache was coming on. Typical for a chat with my family. I'd walked—no, run—away from my ex-boyfriend Edward when I'd learned he'd cheated on me. Keeping him meant turning a blind eye, which I wasn't going to do. Ever. I had plenty of self-respect not to stand for that shit. I'd rather buy a date than be stuck with that loser.

The fact that Edward was going to be the best man only proved no one in my family took how much of an asshole he was into account.

He was in the wedding when I wasn't.

"Astrid, dear." Fuck, my mother was back. "Why do you upset Amy? It's her wedding week."

I didn't say a word.

"To keep the numbers even, I've paired you with Franklin Pierce."

"Franklin? You're kidding," I said, thinking of the guy I'd gone to school with. He'd always been a handsy sort and never shown any interest in me other than I'd had bigger boobs than other girls in my class. The fact that our mothers were friends was the only reason we got thrown together. He worked with his father in a dental practice and the only thing exciting about him was that he shared a name with a former US president.

"Since Edward will be there and you're not together... then I had to find *someone* to be your date."

"For a bachelorette party?"

"It's coed. A joint thing."

I frowned, not sure what that meant. "I have a date, Mother. I'm bringing someone." The words came out unexpectedly. I'd hoped to arrive for the rehearsal dinner solo, stating that since Thatcher ran a bar that he couldn't get away on a Saturday night. He'd show up for the wedding on Sunday and be glued to my side for the service and reception. But now... shit.

There was no backing out now. I had to take Thatcher. It wasn't like I could find another guy in less than a week.

"Really?"

That one word was loaded with questions.

"Yes."

"Well, then. I... well, good."

Good. I'd get Franklin off my back, but now I had to get Thatcher to go with me not just to a Sunday wedding, but an entire weekend. Of family hell.

"Friday, Mother," I finally replied, trying for calm. It was one weekend then I could go back to being ignored. How Amy had landed a fairly decent guy like Michael, I had no idea. Or why he put up with her.

She clicked off before saying goodbye.

"Don't tell me." Mary said, holding up her hand. I'd forgotten she'd heard the whole fun conversation. She was my first and only hire, and also my closest friend. Two years ago, she'd divorced. As a newly single mom of two, she needed income and flexibility and I'd needed help. My business had taken off and while that was a great problem, I'd been working too much. Even with Mary, I still was. "She wants her fancy cake a day early."

I nodded, taking a deep breath and eyeing the wall calendar.

She crossed her arms over her chest, covering the shop logo on her t-shirt. "Now you're going to a bachelorette party?"

"Looks like it," I said with a frown.

"And the cake has to be done for Friday."

"Yup."

She didn't say anything else, just shook her head slowly.

"I know. I know." I turned and picked up the piping bag. Got back to work.

"Take Thatcher with you."

"I have to since I offered him up to my mother so I wouldn't be stuck with Franklin Pierce for the weekend."

She frowned. "Isn't that a former president?"

"Yes!" I said, tossing my hands up, one holding the piping bag.

"You need backup. Support. God, I thought my family was bad. Now I know they're just crazy." She picked up a cloth and folded it.

"He's a fake date," I reminded her. She knew about

Thatcher and how he was going with me. She'd been there when I shared my idea with Aunt Jean about buying a guy from the bachelor auction to go with me and had been at the community center the night before in person. "How am I going to get him to agree to go with me for the entire weekend?"

"A real date—a *good* one—would go with you for support. Know what a nightmare your family is—no offense—and give you lots of orgasms to keep you relaxed."

My eyes bugged out and I started to laugh. "Mary!"

"What? You've got Thatcher Manning as your date. Have you seen him?"

"Uh... yeah." Over six feet of hulking muscle and bodily perfection. Curly ginger hair. Blue eyes. A quick smile that should be considered a lethal weapon to womens' panties.

She fanned herself.

I didn't blame her. He was... incredible. Handsome, a gentleman and after our little chat the night before, a seemingly nice guy. Definitely a little bit of a dirty talker, too, because I'd laid awake thinking about the *extra services* he'd mentioned.

He wasn't really a date. He wouldn't have known who I was if Aunt Jean hadn't won him. I'd shown up late because of a delivery. I hadn't changed my clothes or even swiped on some lip gloss. Hell, I'd had flour on my cheek.

"You *bought* that hot cowboy."

"Aunt Jean did for me." I let my shoulders drop as I felt my self-confidence take a nosedive. "What woman needs her aunt to buy her a date for her sister's wedding?"

She tapped her chin. "Um, a smart one. You aren't the only woman who bought a bachelor last night. I'm sure none of them are complaining. Use Thatcher. For *all* kinds of things."

I picked up the folded towel and threw it at her. "You're insane."

"You're insane not to," she countered, then came over to me, looked me in the eye. "It's going to be a rough weekend, especially now. Ask him to go with you. To all of it."

"He runs a bar and probably can't get away."

"Ask him," she repeated.

"Aunt Jean didn't bid all that—"

"Ask him."

I laughed. "You're not going to stop, are you?"

She shook her head. The bell over the front door jingled, indicating a customer. She left to help, and I got back to work, thinking.

I'd expected to drive to Cutthroat on Saturday night, drop off the cake at the wedding venue and then continue on to the rehearsal dinner. The wedding was at noon on Sunday, so after the reception I'd be able to return to The Bend. I'd only have to spend one night.

Less than twenty-four hours with my family... and others.

I'd dated Edward Klein while I was away at college, meeting him over the summer before my senior year. I'd returned after graduation and learned he'd been cheating on me. Needing to escape, I'd fled to The Bend and Aunt Jean, the only sane blood relation I had. That had been years ago. I hadn't left, instead opened the bakery. I was settled here. Content.

Dateless. I was over Edward but returning to Cutthroat and dealing with my family was hard. Going back and seeing Edward on top of everything else because he was the best man... not fun.

Now I'd have to stay the whole weekend. Mary was right. I needed backup in the form of a red headed hottie. A guy who was nicer—and hotter—than Edward. Glancing at the clock, I wondered when Thatcher would be at the Lucky Spur, because I had some begging to do. Since I told my mother I had a date, there was no way I could show up to the wedding without him now.

4

 HATCHER

IT WASN'T EVEN late and the bar was busy. The weather was good and everyone wanted to be out on the patio by the river. The garage doors I'd put in when I renovated the old mill were open. The band was setting up and the place would fill even more in an hour when they got going. I was helping the bartenders keep up with the orders and while I was focused on the beer I was pulling, my thoughts went to Astrid, as they had all day.

We hadn't talked long after the auction, only solidi-fying that she'd text me later in the week with details about the where and when of her sister's wedding. All I knew was that it was in Cutthroat next Sunday.

I could understand why a woman would want to have a wingman going to an event when an ex was going to be there. I didn't know anything about the guy, but he must've done a number on her. The fact that Miss Turnbuckle was in on it validated that he was an asshole. There was more to this story. But what?

I passed off the beer to a customer and traded it for some cash, then stuck it in the till before taking the next order from a woman dressed in a top that accen-tuated the fact that she wasn't wearing a bra and whose skirt could also be used for a rubber band. She gave me a look that indicated she wanted more from me than a gin and tonic.

On a few occasions in the past, I'd offered a little dick on the side. When I first opened the place, I'd been young and horny. Owning a bar was like shooting fish in a barrel when it came to easy pussy.

This customer was beautiful. They often were. But tonight, I gave her a wink and an extra lime wedge and nothing else.

My mind was on Astrid the baker. Why she made my dick ache, I had no idea. I didn't take her for stupid nor shallow. I wasn't a dick. Just because she didn't wear makeup or flaunt the breasts that God gave her didn't mean she wasn't appealing.

For some reason, she was *too* appealing. That was a problem.

I didn't date. I didn't have relationships. They were too dangerous. Too clingy. Too... everything. I liked things simple. Easy. No strings attached fun.

Because of this, I was totally fine with being Astrid's wingman at her family thing. I could handle an ex. I could tackle a crazy family.

Everyone loved me, but I didn't love in return.

Except my family. No one fucked with them. We Mannings stuck together, but I didn't want a wife or kids. I had a dog, Maple, and she'd had the kids, a big new litter of puppies that made my niece insanely happy.

That was all the procreating that I'd be a part of.

I had a feeling my brothers would be popping out kids soon. I'd learned Sawyer had been bought at the auction by the preschool teacher who had kneed him in the nuts earlier in the week. Even took her for ice cream after the event instead of heading to the store for an athletic cup. If that wasn't love, I had no idea what it was.

Huck had been bought by Sarah O'Banyon and yeah, he was whipped. He'd been that way for years, but it seemed the auction had given him a second chance where she was concerned, even if that included breaking his headboard because she'd been scorned enough to handcuff him to it. He had shit to work through where she was concerned, but a second chance wasn't going to be ignored.

I grinned, thinking about those lovebirds. I refused to be one of them. Alice would have to be satisfied with two out of three of us finding women to keep. I'd say those odds were pretty good results from a charity auction.

"What can I get you?" I asked the next customer, turning and placing a napkin on the bar. When I looked up, it was Astrid. I smiled. "Hey there, sweets."

She smiled in return, pushed her glasses up. She had on jeans and a green, sleeveless top that matched the color of her eyes exactly. The top had little buttons down the front and three of them were undone. Only a hint of cleavage could be seen, but I couldn't miss her shape tonight. My mouth watered at those delectable curves. Full tits, a narrow waist and wide hips. She was like an hourglass with lots of dips and hollows that I wanted to explore. For hours. Days.

"Hi. I know this is a busy time." She glanced around and moved over a little as someone wedged onto the bar stool beside her.

"No worries. I'm glad you stopped by."

I *was* glad. She was... refreshing. That sounded fucking stupid, like she was an ice-cold beer after a hot day mending fences. "Isn't this late for you?"

Nodding, she leaned her forearms on the bar. A little more of her creamy cleavage was revealed. But the fact that she still skipped the makeup and her hair was back in the same braid as the night before meant she wasn't here for seduction. Although the hint of vanilla I breathed in made my dick twitch, which it hadn't done for any of the hot women so far tonight. "I finished the last of my special orders and just picked up a batch of raspberries from McMann's fruit stand. She keeps some on the side for me."

The sun hadn't set yet, but if she was up at four as she'd mentioned, she'd been working well over twelve hours.

I cleared my throat. "What can I get you? Drink? Pillow?"

She grinned, then quirked a brow. "Iced tea?"

I nodded, went to pour that for her. Added a lemon slice. When I placed it in front of her, she pulled out her wallet and I held up my hand. "On me."

She smiled again. "Thanks. I, um..." A rowdy group of guys a few feet down the bar distracted her. "I came to ask you something." Her voice raised to be heard.

I gritted my teeth at the noise. Astrid shouting to talk to me wasn't okay. I looked down the length of the bar and got Kelly's attention. I gave the bar manager a little finger wave to indicate I was stepping away. She nodded and I ducked under the bar flap to get to Astrid. Taking her hand, I said, "Come on."

We weaved through the crowd to my office in the back. I opened the door, gestured for her to enter first, then shut and locked it behind us. She looked around, took in the desk, chair, and file cabinet. It was far from interesting. Intentionally. I did my paperwork here, got shit done, then got the hell out of the bar. When I craved the outdoors, which was pretty much every fucking day, I went home to the ranch. There, I had enough acreage to get lost, which I did often enough. And when I was ready to crash... alone, I had the barn I'd converted into my own place.

I might be heading to Mexico for the winter, but the ranch was—and would always be—home.

"I have a favor to ask. I'm not used to asking for help, but I need it."

I leaned a hip against the edge of my desk, set my hands on the edge. "Shoot."

She bit her plump lip, then looked at me. "I know the auction was for a date and I appreciate you going to my sister's wedding with me."

"But..."

She was nervous about asking this favor. Whatever it was, she thought I wasn't going to like it.

"I'm baking my sister's wedding cake and I just found out I need to deliver it on Friday before the bachelorette party."

I shrugged. No issue there. "Okay. I assumed I'd be driving separately anyway."

She winced. "Yeah, well... My mother paired me with Franklin Pierce since she thought I didn't have a date and I told her I had one because... I do *not* want to be paired with him and—"

"Hold up, sweets." I raised my hand to cut her off. She hadn't taken a breath through any of that. "What the hell is 'paired up'?"

"She found me a date for the entire weekend."

"A former president?"

Her lips twitched and her shoulders relaxed. "I know, right? He's as bad as he sounds." Her mouth dropped and her eyes widened. "Oh shit, I'm sorry. I know you and your brothers are named after Mark Twain characters, but I didn't mean *you* being bad as you sound. I mean, Thatcher's a good name. Huckleberry, too, even though I bake muffins named after him... and the fruit."

I smirked. "It's okay, sweets. I got it. You don't have to worry about hurting my feelings. Or Huck's, for that matter. Ever. I'm good."

She relaxed and a smile curved her lips, although it wasn't as bright as when she was talking about McMann's raspberries.

"Why do you need this ex-president guy? You have a date. Me."

"Yes, and my mother was *very* surprised."

I looked her over trying to figure out why it would be a surprise she was bringing someone.

"Why?"

She frowned. "Why?"

"Why was she surprised? I mean, your ex is the best man so you've dated before. It's not like you just escaped from a convent."

She huffed, then glanced down at herself. "Look at me. God, is that a raspberry stain?" She lifted the hem of her shirt to inspect a red spot. I didn't notice that but instead the strip of skin that was exposed when she did so. Soft, pale flesh just above the top of her jeans.

"Is this ex that much of a catch?"

"Edward?" She set her hands on her hips. "If you like being in a relationship with a two-timer."

I cocked my head to the side and tried to remain calm. "He cheated on you?"

Her eyebrows went up as she nodded.

"Well, he's an asshole."

The guy didn't realize how lucky he'd been. Having a woman like Astrid in his bed but getting some elsewhere? He was stupid, too. I couldn't wait to meet him.

She held up a hand. "Oh, I know it. But my family doesn't."

Clearly, this was a hot button for her. Enough of one that she'd bought a date to take with her. There was enough baggage there for an around-the-world trip and I had a feeling there was a lot she wasn't telling me.

"Your mother doesn't think you can get a date

because you... what, don't get all dolled up on a Saturday night?"

"Pretty much," she admitted, glancing down at herself.

"That's shallow," I told her.

"That's my family," she countered, as if it explained everything.

"Well, they're wrong." I pushed off the desk and she had to tip her head back to keep her gaze on mine. "If a guy doesn't see who you really are because he's caught on a short skirt and a push up bra, then he's not worth your time."

Her mouth fell open, then she snapped it shut. "Says the guy I bought at an auction."

"Says the guy who's going to be your date. Friday to Sunday."

No matter how intriguing I found Astrid, I was probably leaving in a few months. I was settled here in The Bend, but a carefree winter in the tropics? I hadn't officially decided yet, but I had to give him an answer soon. I had a solid bar manager in Kelly. The puppies would be heading to their new homes starting next weekend. If the auction and the short time since was any indication, Sawyer and Huck would be busy fucking their women.

I wasn't getting serious with Astrid or any woman, not if I was leaving town. Hell, not if I was staying either. I didn't do relationships and definitely not long distance. But she was sweet and she seemed as over-loaded with work as me. She needed to have some fun at her sister's wedding instead of it being a chore. For some reason, I wanted to have that fun with her. Besides, it was clear she needed a little help with her family.

"That's what you're here to ask, right?"

She licked her lips. "Yes. Mary, the woman who works with me, says I need a wingman."

If Astrid's mother put parameters around her love for her daughter like it sounded, then Astrid definitely needed backup. I didn't know who Franklin Pierce was, but he wasn't going to get anywhere near her. I doubted I could keep her mother away. That meant I'd have to stick close. *Real* close.

"I'll be your date," I said. "But a guy coming for the weekend is more than just a date."

Her eyes widened and this close, I couldn't miss how green they were. "You mean..."

I grinned. "Sweets, I'm your new fake boyfriend. And if we're going to pull it off, we probably need to practice."

"Practice?"

"Kissing."

5

 STRID

"Um... what?"

He took a step toward me. I stepped back. It was more the predatory, heated look in his eye that had me wary. He wanted to kiss me? *Me?*

The one with flour on her face, a raspberry stain on her shirt who blurted out stupid shit?

I retreated once more and bumped into the closed door. I wasn't afraid of kissing him. The opposite, actually. What if I liked it? God, not *if.* Of course I'd like it. He leaned in, set his forearm beside my head. He was close, so close that every time I took a breath, my breasts brushed his chest. I had to tilt my chin back to look at him and what I saw...

Was he even real? There was something about a ginger, a guy with hair like his. Strands that curled. Untamed, just like Thatcher. His eyes were on mine, mesmerizing in how blue they were. How piercing. The whiskers on his square jaw were more auburn than red and I wondered if they were scratchy. His full lips kicked up at the corner.

"There's no way in hell anyone would believe I'd be able to keep my hands off of you if you were mine."

I blinked.

Thatcher Manning hit all the checkboxes.

Gorgeous. Yes.

Seemingly nice. Yes.

A dirty talker. *Yes,* in that breathy, I'm coming sort of way.

"Or my mouth."

Oh my God.

"I love that you smell like sugar and vanilla. Do you taste just as sweet?"

I wasn't a virgin. I wasn't a prude either. After the auction last night, my vibrator had been put to good use as I thought about Thatcher. Now, I was just... surprised.

A guy like him could have any woman he wanted. Gorgeous ones who left him their numbers on cocktail napkins on a nightly basis. He'd probably collected several tonight alone. And yet he was in his office with the door locked with me.

I'd barely pulled myself together to come here. I'd worked later than I'd wanted and it was either show up... again, without makeup or any kind of cute outfit on my part, or I'd have been too tired to stop by. And I'd had to stop by, to ask if he'd join me for more than Amy's wedding.

A date was one thing, but a *boyfriend*?

I swallowed. Wait. He'd said this plan between us was fake.

That meant he was going to kiss me because a guy like Thatcher had needs a girlfriend would take care of. If I was his *real* girlfriend I'd be more than happy to see to them. Every. Single. One. Especially if it meant he'd taste me.

God, I was stuck on that.

But this was pretend, and I had to stop being flustered and shy around him. He was right. No one at the wedding would buy it. And if they didn't and learned it was all fake, I'd be even more of a loser to them than I already was.

"Well?" he murmured.

"Hmm?"

"Taste sweet."

"I—"

He cut me off with a kiss. Holy hell, a *kiss*.

His lips were firm and warm. Gentle but insistent.

When his hand cupped my cheek... I—what?

There were no thoughts. Nothing was going through my head because all I could focus on was Thatcher's mouth. His fingers sliding into my hair, then wrapping around my braid. The press of his body into mine. The thick prod of his dick in my belly.

I whimpered. Gasped. Made some kind of breathy sound and melted into the door. Thatcher nudged his thigh between mine to hold me up.

I tipped my head back and outright moaned because he bumped my clit.

I'd think about being a wanton hussy later because now I was rolling my hips and riding his thigh, my hands gripping the sides of his shirt and holding him close. A tug on my hair had my mouth opening and his tongue found mine. He didn't taste sweet. Instead, he was minty and dark and wild and... who cared?

We came up for air eventually, Thatcher tipping his forehead against mine as we caught our breath.

When his hand, which was cupping my left boob, gave a little squeeze, I whimpered. Then his thumb slid back and forth once over my hard nipple.

"That was one hell of a fake kiss," I breathed.

"Totally fake."

"Um... the hand on the boob's part of making it believable to my family?" I wondered.

He was so close I could see the dark flecks in his blue eyes. He grinned. "No. That's just for me, sweets."

6

HATCHER

WEDNESDAY

"WHEN CAN Sandy come live with me, Uncle Thatch?"

I was sitting in the stall that we'd turned into the dog nursery. My niece, Claire, was surrounded by puppies. Maple'd had a litter and everyone had been taking care of them. The puppies were now seven weeks old and starting to eat water-softened dog food. They played and rolled around, climbing on Maple, who was getting tired of being stuck with her children twenty-four/seven. I assumed every mother could understand, even the fact that one of them was currently gnawing on her ear and another climbing over her legs.

I petted her head, letting her know she was a good girl. Claire was going to keep one. Since all of them were yellow labs except a single black one, she'd had a tough time keeping which one was hers straight. I had no idea either, but Huck and Sarah had picked out a little pink collar and Claire had put it on one of them the other day. Now she knew which one was hers—even though I'd switched it yesterday because the Sandy she'd picked had turned out to be a boy—and was more eager than ever to take her up to the main house.

"This weekend," I replied.

I had my cell in hand, staring at the text I'd finally gotten back from my friend, Kent. He was the one whose bar I was going to run for the winter in Cozumel.

KENT: Dude, I was in Belize fly fishing. You're in?

I'D TEXTED him five minutes after Astrid left my office on Saturday night. My text had been simple: *I'm in.*

I hadn't heard from him since, until now. In those few days, I hadn't changed my mind about going. In fact, the kiss with Astrid had been the deciding factor. I'd liked it too much and that was a problem. I had a feeling it could lead to more, and I didn't do more. One kiss and my balls had ached all night. I'd had to do bookkeeping at my desk to try to get my dick to go down before I could go back and help the bartenders.

Since Saturday night, Kelsey and Sawyer had gotten together and that was a crazy-as-fuck story. Huck and Sarah were a done deal. Hell, she was already living with him in the main house. I was the last Manning brother standing.

And I was going to stay that way. I texted him back, moving my thumbs over the small screen.

ME: Yes. September to February. Book me a ticket. I'll buy some sunscreen.

KENT: Gonna have to ditch the Stetson.

ME: Not wearing a sombrero.

. . .

I SMILED AT THAT, and I was reassured about my decision. I'd get away from the lovebirds for a while. I stuck my cell back in my pocket, then reached out and snagged a piece of straw from one of the puppies' mouths. "Sandy needs a little more time with her mommy and brothers and sisters," I told Claire.

I leaned against the wood wall, my legs out straight. Horses filled the other stalls in the stable and I'd take one of them out later for a ride.

Claire scooped up Sandy and hugged her close. The puppy wriggled, then licked her face, making her giggle.

It was impossible not to smile at a five-year-old with her first dog.

"Did you get her a dog bed?" I asked.

She looked up from Sandy and shook her head. Her blonde hair was in two short braids that swung back and forth. "She's going to sleep in my bed. And read with me."

I fake frowned. "I thought you read with *me.*"

"You're silly, Uncle Thatch. I also read with Daddy and now Sarah."

While Sarah had her own house downtown, she'd spent every night since she and Huck worked things out here at the ranch. I'd thought Alice would not be thrilled with the two of them sharing a bedroom, but she hadn't said a word. In fact, she'd whisked Claire off on errands often enough so the lovebirds could have alone time.

Like now, Alice had dropped Claire off at my house, the converted barn beyond the stable, saying Huck and Sarah were napping and that Claire could visit with me so the house was quiet. Alice had said that with a miraculously straight face, although she'd given me a wink over Claire's head.

"Daddy loves Sarah."

They'd dated years ago. He'd loved her then. Still did. I was happy for them and Sarah was going to keep my grumpy older brother on his toes. And satisfied in bed. And most likely a daddy again soon enough if they took enough naps.

"I think you're right, Sprout."

"I love Sandy," she added. "What about you?"

I scratched my head. "I love Sandy, too."

Claire rolled her eyes. "No. Do you love the lady person who bought you? Daddy loves Sarah and Seesaw loves Miss Kelsey." Kelsey had been Claire's preschool teacher for a few months. "So you have to love who bought you."

I thought of Astrid. I didn't love her. I barely knew her. But I was intrigued. And that kiss. I shifted in the straw. The soft feel of her body pressed into mine or the way she'd all but melted into the office door as I kissed the hell out of her was all I'd thought about since she'd stopped at the bar. I would see her all weekend and I planned on kissing her again. And more.

I might be a fake boyfriend, but she was into it. Into me. Us. Kissing.

"It doesn't always work out that way," I said.

"What's her name? The lady who bought you."

"Astrid."

"Loving is easy," she replied.

I frowned, but Claire was known for saying confusing things. "What do you mean, Sprout?"

She pursed her little lips as she considered. Then she kissed the top of Sandy's head. "I just love Sandy. I want to keep her forever. She wasn't even borned when there was snow on the ground and now she's going to be mine to keep."

"That's true."

"Seeing her every day, hugging her, it's easy to love her."

She let go of Sandy and the puppy ran off, tumbled with a sibling, then raced back to Claire and flopped down in front of her. "See? Sandy loves me too and she can't even talk."

"Dogs are great to love," I admitted. I loved Maple. "They're always happy to see you and love to give you kisses."

"Daddy loves Sarah. He hugs her all the time. And kisses her."

"True, but they had to work hard to be together."

"Yeah, he said he was working on it, and he did and now she's here. The love part was easy."

In Huck's case, that made sense. For me? Nah.

"And Seesaw?" I asked, calling Sawyer by what Claire had given him when she couldn't pronounce his name properly.

She shrugged her little shoulders. "Miss Kelsey goes into town and Seesaw misses her."

If he were a dog, he'd probably howl with loneliness that she got her own place.

"But he loves her," she added.

"What are you saying?" I asked. "That people leave and it's okay to love them? What does that have to do with me?"

Claire scratched her button nose. "If you hug them and it's easy, then it's love. Even if they go away."

But what if they don't come back?

That was what I wanted to ask Claire, but that was a little deep for a five-year-old. Her grandparents—my parents—had gone away and never came back. They'd climbed into their Piper Cub and crashed, dying instantly.

That had destroyed me. All of us. Huck had taken to loving too deeply, not giving up on Sarah even with a six-year separation. Sawyer had been wanting love, just like Momma and Daddy had. He'd finally found it with Kelsey.

But me? I wasn't going to pick anyone. It was too

risky. The idea of finding a love like my parents and then losing her... I wouldn't be able to handle it. It was better to avoid love.

Safer. That was why I'd considered Kent's offer and definitely why I'd finally said yes.

I thought of Astrid. The kiss we'd shared—it was a hell of a lot more than a hug—had been easy. Amazing. She'd been right there with me even though we both weren't interested in anything serious. I wanted to kiss her again. And again because she felt... like something exciting. Something different. I didn't recognize it or understand it.

I thought of her in the shower when rubbing one out. She'd moved to the prime spank bank fantasy spot. But it was more than that. I thought of her green eyes. The way she blushed. Her smile. Her scent.

Yeah, all those things were why I could be her fake boyfriend for the weekend, but that was it.

I pushed to my feet, brushed straw off the back of my jeans. "Come on, Dr. Ruth. Let's take Maple and the puppies out to the field."

She hopped to her feet. "I'm not Ruth. I'm Claire!" she shouted, then giggled when Sandy and another puppy nipped at her shoelaces.

It was better not to analyze it. Claire's love logic and the fact that I was listening to a five-year-old.

Once outside, Claire ran off, all the puppies

chasing her. Maple went and did her business, then dropped down in the sunshine for a snooze.

Huck and Claire came around the corner hand in hand.

"Done napping?" I asked.

They looked well rested. Or well satisfied.

Huck smirked and Sarah rolled her eyes.

"You still going to Cutthroat this weekend?" Huck asked.

I leaned against the exterior wall of the stable. "Yes."

"Be careful, Thatcher," Sarah said. "Astrid's not like other women."

I pushed off the wall, reached down and snagged a blade of grass. "What other women?"

There wasn't a parade of them coming out of my place doing a walk of shame.

"Exactly."

"What the hell are you talking about?"

Claire got knocked down by one of the puppies and now they were climbing all over her. Her giggling carried on the light breeze. Sarah walked over to her leaving me with Huck.

"You're leaving in two months," he explained. "You told Kent yes." Meaning my winter-long stay in Cozumel.

"And I'm going to what, love Astrid and leave her with a broken heart? She *bought* me."

"Yeah, and look what happened with Kelsey and Sarah."

"You got handcuffed to your headboard and Sawyer got kneed in the balls. Astrid wants me to be her fake boyfriend. Fake. She's set the ground rules with that."

Huck eyed me like he would a suspect, silently waiting for me to crack. I wasn't going to tell him about the smokin' hot kiss or that I wanted to do it again.

"Maybe she's not the one I'm worried about," he said.

"You're worried about me? Why?"

"Why are you going to Mexico?" He'd left off his hat after his *nap* and he ran a hand over his close-cut hair. He and Sawyer looked like our parents. I looked like I was adopted.

I stared at him wide eyed. "Um... Mexico. In the winter. What is there to explain?"

Turning to avoid him, I watched the girls with the puppies. Maple had gone over and was nudging her babies to stay nearby. She was keeping her loved ones close.

I was running away. I wasn't going to tell him that kissing Astrid scared the shit out of me. That the safest place to be where she was concerned was in another country.

"You've got the barn you just finished converting. A bar you love. I'd say you're running away."

I couldn't really argue, so I deflected. "When there's three feet of snow on the ground, think of me in the hot sun and sand between my toes."

"When there's three feet of snow on the ground, I'm going to think about nothing but being inside Sarah."

I instantly thought of Astrid. Which meant I was fucked.

riday

I PULLED into the bakery's small lot and parked my truck. After the little makeout session last Saturday—that was what I was calling it because I'd pulled my hand from Astrid's perfect tit and let her walk out of my office while my dick was hard and dripping pre-cum down the leg of my jeans—we hadn't talked other than her texting me that the wedding wasn't black tie and to meet her here to drive to Cutthroat together.

Astrid was standing at the back of a van that had her bakery logo and Flour Power on the side. The doors were open and a fancy cake sat within. My eyes homed in on her ass. I licked my lips because *that* was what I wanted to take a bite out of. Today she wore a green sundress that only highlighted her wide hips and narrow waist.

It was impossible not to imagine moving in behind her, tossing the hem of her dress up and over her back and bending her forward into her van and taking her hard. I'd watch my dick sink into her pussy, savor the way her ass would sway every time I slapped my hips against it.

Shifting in my seat, I realized none of her relatives would doubt I had a thing for Astrid since my dick was going to be hard all weekend.

The way she'd responded in my office last Saturday meant she was right there with me. The chemistry between us was undeniable—and we'd only kissed, but the rest? She'd bought me at an auction. Bought me.

This was transactional. No strings.

I knew where I stood with her, and it wasn't behind her with my dick in her pussy.

I was her wingman. Her fake boyfriend. That was all.

Right?

If her ex, the stodgy-sounding Edward, had any second thoughts about Astrid, he was going to be sporting a black eye in the wedding photos.

He'd had his chance.

When I'd first agreed, I thought this was going to

be easy. A piece of cake, no pun intended. But as I made my way across the lot to Astrid, I was second guessing that.

When she turned to face me and gave me a huge smile, I was in big trouble. She blushed, hopefully remembering how I'd cupped her breast and played with the hard nipple. It was something I hadn't forgotten, even relived every time I'd been in the shower since. And out.

"Hi," she breathed.

I leaned down and kissed her cheek, tipping my head so my hat didn't bump her. Yeah, fucking vanilla.

"That your sister's cake?"

She peeked at it the way a mother would ensure her child was safely secured in a car seat. "It is. I'd usually put the tiers on after I get there, but Amy wants to see it finished and I won't have time to do the finishing touches later."

"I'm not all that familiar with wedding cakes, but it sure is pretty."

I counted four tiers. White frosting. Flowers all over it in shades of white to pale yellow and pale pink. It was elaborate and... well, impressive.

"Thanks."

"I didn't think you could get flowers that color around here."

"I made them."

Made them?

I took a second glance at the cake. Leaned closer to get a better look, but I knew not to touch. Each petal was curved and angled to perfection. I'd swear they were real. "They're not real?"

"Nope. You can eat them."

Turning, I looked to Astrid. "You're really talented." I wasn't lying. The work she'd done was incredible. The amount of detail and artistry...

She sighed and gave me a pleased look.

"Thanks. Are you ready to go? I don't mean to rush you but while the cake's been in the fridge, I've got to get the van going and the air conditioning running before it softens," she said.

"You're transporting it like that?" I pointed, worried.

She nodded. "Like I said, usually I'd transport each tier in a box and build it at the reception location, finishing off some of the piping and flower work then, but Amy... well, this has dowels in it and should keep it secure. There's a yoga mat underneath so the half box doesn't slip. And as you can see I've built a little area that holds the box in place."

I took in the wooden frame she'd made that kept things from sliding around. Obviously, she'd done this before and knew what she was doing.

Taking my truck wasn't an option. It wasn't like a wedding cake could sit in the pickup truck's open bed.

"I'll grab my bag and we can go."

When I returned, she was opening the driver's door.

"Hang on, sweets," I called, then snagged the keys from her hand when I got close. "I have no problem taking your van, but I'm driving."

She shook her head and glanced toward the back, as if she had Superman eyes and could see the cake inside.

"Unless we're headed to the ER because I'm bleeding out, and maybe even then, I drive my woman around."

She frowned behind her glasses. "Sexist, much?"

I stroked my fingers over her hair. Took in the way it was down her back in thick waves. It was the first time I'd seen it down and it was gorgeous. It was like a chocolate curtain, silky and undeniably sexy. Fuck, she was pretty.

"Nah," I replied. "You've worked hard on that cake and I'm guessing you got up at four. I'm giving you a break. I know you can drive, sweets. Driving is how I take care of you."

"I don't know," she said with some doubt. "The cake—"

"You think I'd drive reckless with you on board?"

Her eyes widened slightly, and she slowly shook her head. "No."

"That's right. The cake will be fine. If he were alive,

my daddy'd kick my ass to Broadwater County if I didn't treat a lady with respect."

She quietly relented and went around to the passenger side, giving me a glance or two as she did so. Hadn't she ever had anyone take care of her before?

I'd normally open the door for her, but she'd already made one concession and didn't want to push it. This time.

It took about ten minutes of driving for Astrid to relax and not dart glances at the cake. I wasn't a crazy driver usually, but now I pretended there wasn't a cake in the back but a big bowl of gravy that I didn't want to spill. The idea of damaging the cake she'd made to such perfection for what sounded like a bridezilla sister made my palms sweat. Not that I'd tell her that. Ever.

"I'm surprised you're walking away from your business for the weekend."

Out of the corner of my eye, I caught an eye roll. "It's not easy to do, that's for sure. Mary, my assistant, is covering, and I trust her. I double baked this morning so there will be enough for the weekend."

I didn't know exactly what that meant, other than she'd been up since before dawn and was still awake. That was impressive in itself.

"You want to tell me about your family and what I'm walking into?" I asked, switching topics.

Cutthroat was a little over an hour from The Bend and we had some time on our hands.

The air conditioner was cranked and I wanted to send out a thank you to the inventor because Astrid's nipples were poking against the soft fabric of her dress. I remembered how responsive one had been beneath my thumb.

"It might be better going in blind."

"Why's that?" I asked.

She glanced at me, then fiddled with her fingers. "Some families are crazy. Loving, but insane. Mine are... mine."

That explained nothing, but if she wasn't in the wedding party because she didn't fit into a dress, then I had a feeling she was following the rule of *if you don't have anything nice to say, don't say anything at all.*

As for bridesmaid dress not fitting, I had no idea what kind of weird-ass style the ladies would wear, but Astrid fit perfectly in the one she had on. It was sleeveless, the green the same color as her eyes. The neckline dipped in a V accenting her large breasts, but not flaunting them. A slim shiny black belt circled her waist which made the flirty skirt flare out. It rode up a little since she was sitting, and the peek of bare thigh made my mouth dry. Combining all that with cowgirl boots, she was fucking gorgeous. Simple and understated, but she didn't need flashy. Today she had a hint of makeup on. There was definitely something shiny on her lips which I wanted to smudge and kiss right off.

Hell, I wanted to tell her to flip up the hem of her dress and show me the color of her panties, but... *fake boyfriend.*

I cleared my throat and wondered if the air conditioning could go any lower. "How about a brief rundown."

She sighed. "Sure. There's my mom and dad. My father is a doctor. Cardiology. My mother is a stay-at-home mom, even though I moved out when I went to college. Amy, my sister, is two years older than me and still lives with them. She's marrying a guy from the country club. Michael. He's an accountant. There's Edward, my ex. Then friends of Amy and Michael I'm sure we'll meet tonight for the coed bachelor/bachelorette party."

"Miss Turnbuckle's your great-aunt, so will she be coming to the wedding?"

She nodded, then tucked her hair behind her ear. I wanted to get my fingers tangled in those long tresses. Tug her head back and—

"On Sunday, yes. She's my father's aunt."

"No others?" I wondered.

"There are a few more relatives coming. No one worth mentioning, although it is my plan after I drop off the cake that I have a drink in hand all the way until we leave on Sunday."

"The wedding and reception is at a hotel?"

A beep came from her purse and she pulled out her cell, read a text and responded with a flurry of moving thumbs.

"Sorry, my sister. Yes, the hotel overlooks the ski resort. The view is pretty."

"Not your type of thing?" I asked. If she was from Cutthroat and her daddy was a doctor, her family had some big bucks. The Manning family wasn't hurting. Hell, I didn't have to work at all, but then what would I do with myself? We just didn't flaunt it. I had a feeling Astrid's family might be the opposite.

"The last thing I want at my wedding is a big cake. Or it taking place in Cutthroat. In fact, I can't really see it at all. What about you?"

"Me? Get married?" I laughed and kept my eyes on the road. "Huck will most likely be hitched before first frost." Probably get Sarah pregnant by then, too. Claire wouldn't stop talking about how Sarah was her new mommy and neither she nor Huck were telling her otherwise. Alice had been walking around in a cloud of happiness. "Sawyer by next summer, if he has his way."

"You didn't answer, you know," she countered, then set her hand briefly on my upper arm. "Don't panic. The secret word of the weekend is *fake*. I know you're not my real boyfriend and I'm not planning on wrangling you into a relationship, let alone a marriage."

"You don't want true love?" I arched a brow in her direction.

She laughed. "Let's have this talk *after* you meet my family."

She didn't want to get married because her family was most likely nuts. I didn't want to get married because my parents had died. I still missed them. I didn't even understand how Astrid could be so distant with hers.

"Well, we do the bachelorette thing and go upstairs to our room at the hotel to sleep," I replied, simplifying it down.

She didn't answer, so I looked her way. Her teeth bit down into her lower lip and she twisted her fingers about. I carefully slowed the van and pulled over.

She looked around. "Why are we stopping here?"

"You look as if I'm driving you to get your wisdom teeth pulled."

Her shoulders dropped when she sighed.

"I know how to relax you."

She frowned, then blushed.

I grinned.

"Not quite that," I added, catching on to where her mind had gone. "A kiss."

"Oh."

"Totally fake." I tossed that out there just so she knew there was no pressure. Reaching over, I stroked her hair back, amazed at the thick curtain. "I love your hair like this." I didn't give her a chance to respond. Just kissed her. I didn't linger. Not since we were on the side of the road. We had a time sensitive cake in the back.

I lifted my head, then gently pressed her glasses into place.

I felt triumphant that she looked *much* more relaxed. If I had some time, and a bed, I could make her boneless. And I wouldn't have a hard dick and blue balls.

Yet I was kicking myself for giving in. Her lips seemed to be my weakness. She'd just said this was fake, reassuring me she wasn't trapping me into something. I was the one who was putting the moves on, which was what I wanted. But didn't want.

Fuck! I wanted Astrid but didn't want commitment. She was giving that to me so why was I insane?

"The thing is..." she began. "We're not staying at the hotel. We're staying with my parents."

What the—

I was thirty years old and I was going to be sleeping in my pretend girlfriend's house with her parents down the hall. This just got better and better.

"Then *I* sure as shit need another fake kiss. That one was for you. This one's for me," I replied, taking her lips once more. Adding tongue and tugging at her hair as I wanted.

I finally pulled back onto the road and we didn't

say much after that. I was trying to figure out why a kiss with Astrid was better than sex with any woman I could remember.

I stared at the road for a bit, the silence between us easy. When I looked over at her next, she was asleep, her head tipped to the side. Her dark lashes fanned over her cheeks and her hair swept over her bare shoulders.

She was sure fucking pretty.

Thirty minutes later, I pulled in front of the hotel where we were dropping off the cake. I'd been to Cutthroat before. While it was bigger than The Bend, I knew my way around. Two women, clearly a mother and daughter pair, stood in matching poses of arms crossed and tapping right feet.

I tapped her on the shoulder and her eyes opened.

"Sorry. I can fall asleep anywhere."

"No worries," I replied, then tipped my chin out the front window. "I assume you know them."

"My mother and sister," she replied, her voice grim.

The welcome wagon didn't look all that welcome. They looked... put out. We were bringing the prettiest wedding cake I'd ever seen. I blew out a breath and realized this was probably going to get far, far worse. A kiss wasn't going to be enough. For either of us.

 STRID

"IT'S LOVELY, DEAR," my mother said.

I'd kissed her and Amy on their cheeks, then opened the back of the van so they could see the cake. They were way more interested in that than me. I took in their summer dresses and high heels, their styled hair and artfully applied makeup.

I wasn't a schlump, but I felt like one whenever we were together. Weight and height aside, my dress was from a secondhand store in The Bend. I'd chosen cowgirl boots instead of teetering on toothpicks. I wasn't skilled at hairstyles. Working with food made braiding my hair a daily requirement and found leaving it down was a treat. As for makeup, I spent ten minutes on a good day "putting on my face" but preferred colored lip gloss over the more potent shades Amy preferred.

"I expected it to be larger," Amy commented, breaking me from my thoughts.

Bigger?

"It's a four-tier cake that can feed two hundred. How much bigger should it be?" I countered.

Hours had been spent on this cake. First were the drawings, the back and forth with Amy on everything from shape to flavor to decorations. I'd baked the layers last weekend, kept them chilled in the fridge and began the decorating on Monday. There were over twenty sticks of butter in the thing between the batter and the frosting. I had a feeling if either of them knew that, they wouldn't take a bite. I'd hand made over one hundred roses, lilac, and lily of the valley accents. I'd texted her pictures of the work-in-progress.

"I just wanted it to make a *grand* statement, just like me," Amy added.

I turned and looked her over. We had the same brown hair, but that was where our similarities ended. Where I was short, she had five inches on me. I had trouble finding bras that fit well *and* looked pretty. Amy didn't even need an underwire. She weighed a hundred and ten pounds soaking wet and flaunted a size two figure. My *thigh* was that size.

She wore a slim dress that fell to just above her knee. The bright yellow made her hard to miss, but with her strappy high heels, she looked elegant and sexy. The huge diamonds in her ears and in the engagement ring on her finger made her look expensive. A guy could take one look at her and know she was high maintenance and costly to keep happy.

I could tolerate her being taller and prettier. I'd been used to that my entire life. It was her *grand* attitude she carried around like a designer purse that drove me bonkers. She didn't even notice how the flowers perfectly matched the photo of what her bouquet would include, which she'd been adamant about. Or the color, a slightly deeper shade of off-white to match the "bone" color of her dress.

Mother looked equally elegant in her blue dress, but it wasn't sexy or flashy. She went for understated, except for her jewelry which was big, shiny, and plentiful.

"You wouldn't want a cake to overshadow the bride."

At the sound of Thatcher's voice, Amy and Mother spun about on their three-inch heels.

I bit my lip at the look on their faces. Amy's eyes widened to saucers and my mother's mouth dropped open like a fish.

Thatcher definitely had that effect on women.

Young and old. And in crisp jeans, a white snap shirt and cowboy hat, he was... devastating.

"*You're* Astrid's date?" Amy asked, as if the idea couldn't be possible.

I bristled worse than her passive aggressiveness about the cake.

"From what Astrid has told me, you're her sister, Amy," he countered.

I thought about everything I'd told him about my sister, which wasn't much.

"Astrid, dear," Mother said, talking to me but eyeing Thatcher. "Aren't you going to introduce us?"

Thatcher tipped his hat. "Thatcher Manning, ma'am."

I winced as Mother hated being called ma'am since it reminded her she wasn't twenty-five any longer. His effect was clearly strong on her since she didn't say a word.

A woman approached, a big confident smile on her face. She was in simple black pants and a white blouse. Subtle and understated. "Hey there. I'm Kit Lancaster, the wedding planner. I saw your van and can't wait to see the cake."

I'd talked to her on the phone this week about the hotel's fridge space to store the cake, but I swept my arm out welcoming her to take a peek.

"Oh, it's gorgeous!" She looked thrilled. *This* was what I was hoping for from my sister.

"I'm sure you want to get this gorgeous cake in the kitchen's fridge before it melts," Thatcher commented.

"Got some helpers right here," Kit added, then turned her head and waved two men in white uniforms over. Mother and Astrid stepped out of the way and I gave quick directions to them on how to handle the cake. "Nice to meet you, Astrid. I'll take care of this beauty for you."

They whisked it away and then I was stuck with nothing to do except spend the weekend with my family.

Oh joy. Kit was too efficient.

"Astrid, you'll want to take your van away as soon as possible," Mother advised. It wasn't good to have it known one of her children worked in the service industry, even though she was the one who wanted me to make the cake.

Before I could respond, Mother glanced at her watch. "Oh, look at the time. I don't know why you always decide to be late, but the coed party has already started."

She looked me over and her lips pinched. This was why they didn't look thrilled when we'd pulled up. Well, *one* of the reasons. They hated it when I came in the bakery van. It was the only vehicle I had. Not only did it offer constant advertising, it made no sense for me to drive something else when I was paying for this one.

Since Amy had told me to arrive at seven and they were out front waiting at this exact time, she was just being... herself. Then again, I wasn't sure why Amy had told me to come now when I was late to tonight's party.

"I am always punctual, Mother," I reminded.

"And if she was a bit late, that's a woman's prerogative, right?" Thatcher added, setting his hand on my shoulder and kissing my temple. The gesture was reassuring and felt dang good.

Mother stared. Amy stared.

"That... that doesn't give you time to change or put your contacts in, but at least you're here."

"Yes, I'm here," I replied. "As requested. This is what I'm wearing, and you are well aware that contacts bother me." I had no idea what she wanted me to change into or why my glasses were a bother. It wasn't like I was wearing Mickey Mouse ears or something. Or my bakery t-shirt.

She pursed her lips. "When you said you were bringing your boyfriend, Astrid, I didn't realize you were bringing someone so—"

"Thatcher," I cut her off, petrified with how she was going to finish that sentence. "This is my Mother, Patricia, and my sister, Amy."

"Ladies. Congratulations to you on such a happy event."

Both of them practically preened at his words.

"I see Astrid's beauty runs in the family," he added.

They frowned, as if he'd totally stumped them.

Mother pulled herself together first. "The party is tonight, here in the bar, then there's softball tomorrow after lunch, then the rehearsal dinner and the wedding Sunday," Amy added.

Softball? I hadn't heard of that one, especially since the only sport Amy ever played growing up was competitive clothes shopping. Fortunately, I always packed casual clothes and a sports bra whenever I traveled so I'd be able to play without getting two black eyes—and making a fool of myself in the process.

As for the rest of the weekend's wardrobe, I had yet to see the dress for Sunday. Perhaps "being late" saved me from that tonight.

"I'll park the van if you ladies want to go inside," Thatcher offered.

I nodded and he gave my shoulder a squeeze before closing the van's back doors. Amy hooked her arm through mine and led me up the front entry steps of the country club as she glanced over her shoulder as Thatcher drove off.

"I want to know everything about him," she said. "*Everything.*"

"He's just a guy, Amy," I countered.

"Have you seen him? I mean, he wears a cowboy hat."

"Um, yeah, I've seen him," I replied. I couldn't miss

the cowboy hat because it had a serious effect on me. It seemed to have one on Amy, too.

"Don't be petty," she snapped. "Share. He's big. Is he big... everywhere?" She waggled her eyebrows and gave me a sly grin.

I tried so hard not to blush, which was easily tempered by anger.

"Aren't you getting married this weekend?" I countered. "To Michael? The guy whose *everywhere* you should be thinking about?"

She huffed, but said nothing more.

We cut through the fancy central hallway to the bar that overlooked the eighteenth hole. It was clear today and the top of Cutthroat Mountain was visible, snow still capping the tall peak. The club had a look of the Wild Wild West crossed with stodgy boarding school. There were elk and moose heads on the walls along with marble floors and gaudy red carpet. Cutthroat was known for its ski resort that catered to the wealthy and bored. Golf clubs replaced skis in the summer. My parents had been members my whole life and I recognized some faces we passed, including those who worked here.

Thatcher caught up to me at the bar. The server was handing over my glass of wine.

"Sorry," I said.

He set his hand on the small of my back and ordered a glass of ice water. "For what?"

I looked up at him. "My sister and mother. I swear they were drooling."

He grinned and I needed a cocktail napkin myself. "Warm enough?" he asked.

The club was air conditioned, even though it was rarely needed. The weather today was in the seventies.

"Yes, thanks."

He nodded, then his gaze lowered to my chest. "It's cooler here and I just wanted to make sure."

I smacked him on the arm when he'd picked up on the fact that my nipples were hard. The blush alone warmed me up. So did his smile. What he didn't know was they weren't diamond points because of the cooler air at high altitude, but all due to him. As soon as he was near, they tried to reach out and get to him.

"Glad I've got an effect on you."

Boy, did he ever.

"What exactly is a coed bachelor/bachelorette party?" he asked, thankfully changing the subject.

I scanned the room. The mahogany bar ran the length of the back wall. There were high-top tables in a row in front of it, then small tables with comfortable chairs spread out around the room. For the private event, there was a banquet table covered in hors d'oeuvres and snacks. I counted about thirty people mingling and chatting.

"I think it's just a cocktail party."

"So no male strippers or women popping out of a cake."

My eyebrows went up and took a second to imagine that happening in this stodgy bar.

"Doubtful. Although most of them will be drunk by nine. Who knows what will happen then." I pointed to a group of men most likely talking about their golf game based on their body motions. "You ready for this weekend's lineup?"

"Go for it."

"The one with the gray hair and green shirt is my dad." As if he'd heard me talking about him, he looked our way, smiled and offered a little wave.

"You get along with him?"

I knew he asked because it was clear I only tolerated Amy and Mother.

"It's hard to say when he's worked sixty-hour weeks since 1985," I replied, then looked up at him because my father had gone back to chatting with his friends. "I always wondered how he and my mother fell in love, or how he'd stayed with her all these years."

"Why's that?"

"At this point, I'd say it's a marriage of convenience. He makes the money and she spends it. He works all the time or is here at the club. She shops."

"Amy does too?"

"Absolutely. Fortunately for her, Michael's rich."

I remembered then that the Manning's weren't

poor either. Their huge property was well known in The Bend. So were the three brothers. I knew Alice, their housekeeper, from the strawberry shortcake.

"Sorry, I sound petty."

He shrugged. "Money does weird things to people," he countered.

"Not me. I have a trust, which you probably didn't even need to know about, but I don't touch it. I went to college on a scholarship. I live off what the bakery brings in."

"Because you don't want to be like them?"

I nodded and looked at the snap on his shirt.

"Sweets, I've only just met them, but I feel confident in saying you couldn't be like them if you tried. Are you sure you weren't born in a cabbage patch?"

I snorted, then laughed so loud that heads turned our way.

"Stork," I countered. "Anyway, I think my parents' love, or lack of it, is why I'm still single. Amy and Michael are on their way to being just like them, and they haven't even said 'I do' yet."

What could he say to that? I redirected the conversation, realizing I was sharing things that Thatcher probably didn't care about.

Fake boyfriend. Even if he were a real date, no guy wanted to hear about how fucked up my family was. He didn't need the words. He could see it for himself.

I directed him to a cluster of younger guys by the

bar. "The one in the pants with anchors embroidered on them is Michael, my future brother-in-law. Besides his odd taste in fashion, he's a nice guy."

"Dad's name?"

"Charles."

"Michael and Charles. Got it. Which one's the former president?"

I grinned. "Franklin Pierce is the blond guy to Michael's left."

"The guy beside him is Thomas Bunker," he said, which had me looking from the group of guys, to him, surprised.

His jaw was clenched.

"That's right," I agreed. "You know him?"

"He's from The Bend. My brothers and I grew up with Bunky. His wife's sister is Huck's woman."

"From the tone of your voice, you don't like him," I said.

"He's an asshole," he muttered.

"He's in Amy's circle of friends. They went to college together. I think his grandparents invented something and he's loaded, which is most likely why they're still close."

"And why he fits in here."

"Astrid! Jello shots!" We turned at Amy's shout. She waved me—with her other hand holding up an orange filled shot glass—over to a cluster of women who surrounded her and were all eyeing Thatcher. A waiter stood by with more shots on a tray.

I gave her a little wave and leaned toward Thatcher. "You know Amy. With her are the bridesmaids, plus a few other friends. A cousin from Seattle. I can give you all their names if you—"

"Astrid."

This time the voice calling me was male. And much closer.

Thatcher and I turned as one.

"Edward," I said, my voice practically a whisper. I took a big swig of my wine. I knew seeing my ex was unavoidable, but I'd hoped to hold off at least a few minutes.

He leaned in to kiss my cheek but I turned my head away so he got a mouthful of hair before he pulled back.

"Thatcher Manning." Thatcher stuck his hand out.

Edward blinked, then was forced by good manners to shake, but recognized a block when he saw one. "Edward Klein."

My heart was pounding and my palms were damp. I hadn't seen Edward since a holiday party a few years ago. Living in a different town made it easy to avoid him, but Mother often updated me on his life. Sadly.

"You look good," Edward told me. "I guess the bakery's doing well."

I bristled at the subtle insult. I might taste my products, but I didn't eat the entire case. It was bad to eat the profits. How had I dated him for almost a year?

"You look... the same," I replied. He did look good. For him. But next to Thatcher, his flaws were obvious. He was short with a paunch and his hair was receding. It wasn't that other men with those attributes weren't nice, but it was the fact that he was a cheater that put him in the asshole category.

Where both men spent lots of time outdoors, Edward did it in khakis and golf shirt with a five iron in his hand. Thatcher might own a bar, but it was obvious —and I didn't mean because of the Stetson on his head —that he was *all* cowboy.

"This your ex?" Thatcher asked, his voice even.

I blushed and murmured my assent as I took another sip of wine.

Surprising me, and Edward, Thatcher reached out and slapped him on the shoulder. "I want to thank you, Eddie."

"Edward," he countered, but Thatcher ignored him.

"You being such a dipshit made it easy for Astrid to recognize a decent guy when I came along."

I choked on my next sip. Thatcher turned to me, stroked my back. "You okay, sweets?"

I nodded, stunned. He'd stood up for me. He'd put Edward... *Eddie,* in his place. My mother hadn't, only wondered why I couldn't make him happy enough not to cheat. My sister didn't understand why I'd walked away from his bank account. My father hadn't said anything, which was his M.O.

But Thatcher... he didn't have to do that. It wasn't in the fake boyfriend job description. But he had.

"I think your sister called for you," he added. "You ready to go hang with the ladies?"

Looking between the two of them, the guy who'd gotten in my pants but was an asshole and the guy I *wanted* in my pants who wasn't.

"Don't worry about me. Eddie and I are going to get to know each other. Right, Eddie?"

Amy rushed over, looking a little panicked, which made no sense. "Edward, give the lovebirds a little room."

Edward wasn't smiling. In fact, his face was blotchy red and he turned and fled.

I tried not to smile but it was really hard.

Amy tugged on my hand. "Come on. Let's have some fun."

"Be right there," I said.

After one glance toward Edward who was now waving down the bartender, she walked off. Thatcher set his hands on my shoulders and leaned down so he looked me straight in the eye. "You good?"

I nodded, clutching my wine glass. "You didn't have to do that."

"Yes, I did," he countered immediately.

I felt a rush of emotion, of pleasure, and not the sexual kind. Okay, that kind too, but I felt... protected. As if he was taking care of my problems for me. Or at least shielding me from them.

It was impossible to look anywhere but at those blue depths. "I've been thinking about that kiss," he admitted, Edward forgotten.

That kiss. "Oh?"

"Yeah, I want another."

My eyeballs flicked left and right as if watching a tennis match. "This isn't exactly—"

He didn't let me say more but took my mouth. It wasn't a little peck, but full-on PDA most likely not seen in the country club. Ever.

His arms went around me, and I was tipped back. He grabbed the wine glass from me as his tongue met mine. The kiss didn't last long, but he was thorough.

"You good?" he asked again when he set me back on my feet, this time for a completely different reason.

"Holy shit," I muttered. My brain cells were scrambled. My nipples were trying to work their way out of my bra and dress to get to him and my pussy was wanting me to find the nearest service closet.

"Yeah, you're one hell of a fake kisser," he said. "I'll be here if you need me."

"Right," I replied, remembering myself. "The fake boyfriend."

"I'm not a good option, sweets. I'm headed to Mexico for the winter."

His words were surprising, not only because they caught me off guard, but he was reminding me he was doing his job. Being a *fake* boyfriend and nothing more. But it felt like one hell of a *real* kiss.

"Right. Sure. Don't worry. I know the deal. It's all for show."

As he stroked a hand down my hair, he added, "Watch out for those jello shots."

He set my wine back in my hand and turned me around to face the women, who were openly staring. With a little pat on my bottom, he pushed me in their direction. When I glanced over my shoulder, he winked, then tipped his hat.

Fake boyfriend. *Fake boyfriend.*

When Amy and her friends swarmed around me, peppering me with questions about my hot man and whether he had any brothers, I couldn't help but smile. Right now, I wasn't the overweight younger sister. I was the one with the hottest guy in the room who'd just kissed my lip gloss right off. And they were jealous.

It felt good to have something the others envied instead of pitied—because they all knew the history between me and Edward and had most likely showed up hoping to see how I'd mope and pander for his attention. Instead, they saw that I was desirable to a guy like Thatcher. That he was practically eye fucking me from the bar.

Except it wasn't real. He'd done what I needed. Handled my mother like a pro. Dealt with Edward. *Eddie.*

Made it very clear we were together. Except we weren't. It was all fake. His protectiveness. His chivalry. His interest. All of it. Because this was a weekend thing no matter what my pussy was telling me. Mary had told me to sleep with him anyway. If it was only for the weekend, I should get my money's worth. And my pussy was thinking Thatcher Manning was *very* worth it.

Mary would jump him. Amy was ready to do so, even though she was the bride. Even Aunt Jean had said she'd do him if she were fifty years younger. Maybe I should. I grabbed another wine from a passing waiter, skipping the shots. If I couldn't get enough nerve to buy him at the bachelor auction, I was going to need some liquid courage to jump him.

 HATCHER

I'D MET some dipshits in my day, but Eddie wore the crown of that kingdom. He'd screwed around on Astrid.

Astrid.

I was just getting to know her, but I'd bet my right nut she'd never, ever, cheat on a guy. She didn't have it in her. She was too loyal, too... good.

She was also hot as fuck. Funny. Tempting. The women that surrounded her were pretty, but they had nothing on her. That green dress made her stand out. Her long hair made me want to wrap it around my fingers and tug her head back as I fucked her from behind. And that ass... it made me think of very dirty things I wanted to do to the woman.

I wanted her to have something else smudged across her cheek besides flour. Sprayed across those plump tits. Marking her pussy.

My tongue flicked out to lick Astrid's taste off my lip. And what the fuck flavor was her lipstick? Cherry?

I'd had to tell her about Mexico. Now that she knew I was leaving, that for me this really was just a weekend thing to help her, I could breathe easier. Kiss her without consequences.

And that was one hell of a kiss.

The only thing that kept my dick from breaking through my zipper was having to look at Eddie's face. And the only thing keeping me from punching him for cheating on Astrid... and for her giving him consent to touch her body when they were together, was Astrid herself.

She'd given herself to him willingly. A gift. And he'd tossed it aside as if it were trash.

I might want to do dirty things to her, but at least I'd put her first. I'd make her want every single one of those dirty things. And love it.

I'd never look at another woman if she were mine.

I didn't give a shit about the fancy country club setting or the pretentious people who would be witness to giving Eddie what he deserved. I didn't want anything I did to reflect on her because she had enough shit to deal with this weekend.

I had to wonder if these guys were real. Who the hell wore khakis in Montana? As I glanced around, almost all the men wore them. Fuck me, Cutthroat was a crazy town.

"Can I get a whiskey?" I asked the bartender, realizing I'd need more than water to make it through the event. I never usually drank because running a bar had ruined it for me. Except I was going to need a little fortification to handle this fuck show. I'd still be able to keep an eye on Astrid, protect her from her ruthless family, acquaintances, and Amy's—and most likely Michael's—friends.

These were the people she'd grown up around? Who she'd chosen to be with?

Eddie the cheating fuck? Amy who had been eyeing me like I was a piece man candy she wanted to suck. No, Astrid had walked away from Eddie years ago. Ditched Cutthroat all together for The Bend and her aunt, Miss Turnbuckle, seemingly the only level-headed one in her crazy family.

My cell vibrated in my pocket. I read the screen. A text from Kent.

KENT: *Can you come a week early?*

. . .

SHIT. In Cozumel I'd have to deal with a bunch of drunk assholes, but I'd take their money and ensure they got in a cab. I wouldn't have to mingle and chat. It would be easy. But empty. I'd have sun and sand. And no one like Astrid to kiss.

That wasn't true. There were probably tons of women who I could get into my bed. Mexicans. Americans. Tourists from countries all over the world came to Cozumel for a little fun. They could have some with me.

The shrill screams of the women had me looking their way. Astrid stood with them, laughing. In the past the idea of a weekend of fun with a random lady made my dick stir. The idea now seemed... boring. Astrid's lips were like honey. Her curves like a roadmap to heaven. That smile, like lightning in a storm. Exhilarating and blinding.

I sounded like an idiot, which meant being with Astrid was fucking with me.

I worried about her. Eddie was a fuckwad and being here was a social landmine. One false move and someone would explode.

I'd respond to Kent later, because this weekend, it was my job to ensure it wasn't Astrid because I could easily seeing her lose her shit. Yeah, she needed to take a load off. Take a break and more than the nap she'd had in the van. If the wedding cake she'd made for her sister was any indication of her work, and work ethic, then she needed to let loose a little. She'd already let her hair down, at my dick's expense, and she deserved some fun. I wasn't sure how she was going to do it with this crowd, but she sure looked like she was trying. Maybe it was easier when she already expected them to be assholes or women with their claws out.

No wonder she'd gotten Miss Turnbuckle to buy me at an auction. Going into this alone would have been a nightmare. I could handle it because I wasn't emotionally invested, but this was her family. Her people.

Well, maybe not *her* people. Because Eddie was a waste of space. I knew nothing about Franklin Pierce, but if all her mother thought him good for was to be paired up with her daughter, then he was a dud. All the other guys in the room too.

None of them knew the real Astrid, or wanted to. They were here for her bird-bones sister.

This was Cutthroat. It was all about money. Status. Petty shit. How I knew this for a fact was that Bunky was here. If there was a picture beside the definition of a stuck-up asshole in the dictionary, it would be his. Thomas Bunker lived in The Bend and thought his shit didn't stink. His name had come up a time or two at home in the past week. Sawyer and Kelsey both discovered Bunky was Kelsey's ex from Colorado. It was a long story, but it meant Bunky wasn't just a little shit, he was a lying cheater on top of it. His wife, Lynn, was mingling now with the ladies, meaning she either had no clue to his philandering, which I doubted, or she didn't care. To make things even worse, Lynn was Sarah O'Banyon's sister, so when Sarah and Huck got married, we'd all probably see the guy more than we ever wanted. God, I hoped they'd elope.

Eddie had been the kickoff guy for the night.

"You're my daughter's boyfriend."

I turned at the voice and pushed Bunky from my mind. This was Astrid's father. Yeah, he was fucking next up.

"Thatcher." I stuck my hand out for him to shake.

"Charles."

"What are your intentions toward my daughter?"

I arched a brow because I thought that question was only in movies. "She's almost thirty years old. I wasn't aware she had to defer to her father in these matters."

Her age was something I didn't know, but I wasn't going to tell him that.

He ignored me and asked, "Are you employed?"

"I own a bar in The Bend."

"So you want Astrid for her money."

I clenched my jaw and counted to three. No ten.

The first thing that came to mind was that I wanted Astrid for her tits and pussy, but I wasn't going to say that. Instead, I told him, "She has other attributes that I find appealing." And I meant *more* than T and A. I was a guy. I loved her breasts, but I also loved how she pushed her glasses up her nose when she was nervous. Or how I could get her to blush.

He narrowed his eyes, even cocked his head to the side. For a guy around sixty, he was fit. No gut, no jowls. Maybe it was because he was a cardiologist and didn't want to drop dead on the links like his patients.

"Right."

I took off my hat, ran a hand over the back of my neck. He didn't think Astrid had anything to offer a relationship besides money?

After meeting her sister, I could see why he might think that. But Astrid and Amy couldn't be any different.

I didn't like to toss around my last name. It was pretty well known in this part of Montana, but I didn't give a fuck what people thought of me. If he assumed I was a simple bar owner, that was fine by me. Whatever.

I sure as fuck didn't want an in with this guy because I had a big ranch and a bigger bank account.

"I'm the lucky one," I added. "A strong woman like Astrid doesn't need a guy. She's a successful business-woman. Talented."

He raised his hand, flagged down the bartender. Waggled his finger to signal another round.

"I saw you met Edward," he added. "Why she broke up with him, I'll never understand."

"Perhaps because he's a cheating asshole," I replied.

His eyebrows went up, then he tipped his head and laughed. I wasn't sure if he was amused by my response or thought it ridiculous since the fucker was the best man. I assumed Charles was paying for this shindig and the ones to follow later this weekend.

"Astrid won't have to worry about him while she's here," I told him, making that clear. If he took it as a threat, so be it. Eddie was out of her life. I was in it.

Shit. Was I? *Fake* boyfriend.

She had to deal with these fruitcakes all the time. Weddings, holidays. She needed a wingman longer than a weekend. Strangely enough, I wanted to take care of her. To watch out for her. Stand up for her when it seemed no one else would.

He looked me over, assessing my value, then slapped me on the shoulder. "Good. But your relationship's new. Trust me. Give it time and you'll be thinking differently." Leaning close, he continued. "The real bachelor party's happening later, after the ladies clear out. Edward's got a few strippers showing up to give Michael a real send-off. Stick around and get a real lay in before you head back to the house."

Charles was a piece of work. He was offering me a hooker before I climbed in bed with his daughter. No wonder he didn't give a shit about what Eddie had done or having him be the best man. He favored the fucker over his own daughter.

Why would I want a woman who probably had fake tits and fake orgasms when I'd come here with the most real woman I'd met in a while? Astrid didn't try to get people to like her. She didn't try to make herself beautiful. She just was. Maybe that was what drew me to her. No, it was definitely her perfect tits, but I was here because of her. Because I wanted to see her smile. I wanted to make her blush. I wanted to know what color her panties were. I wanted her to show me. I wouldn't take. I wanted her to give. That meant I had to give too, which was fucking hard.

It meant putting myself out there. Committing, even for a short time, which I didn't do. Except with Astrid, I wanted to be there for her. I wanted to be the guy she looked for across the room. The one who she told her secrets. Who let me see how fucking dysfunctional her family was.

Charles guided me toward the other men—Bunky and Eddie included—and I tossed back what was left of my whiskey. He slapped Bunky on the back. "Thomas, impressed you pulled yourself from the casino. Win that cash back yet?"

Bunky blanched and took a big swig of his drink.

"Bunky," I said as greeting.

Bunky tipped his chin, then bolted like a rabbit freed from a snare.

I could breathe easier with him trying to avoid me.

While this was forty-eight hours of insanity, that's all it was. Astrid and I would part ways after the wedding reception. I'd drive her back to The Bend, kiss her cheek—maybe her mouth—and it would be Date Over. Astrid had the fake boyfriend she needed. I was the nice guy who helped out. Miss Turnbuckle would definitely keep me first in line for any great new book.

The next time I did something like this, I'd ask the woman why she needed a fake date. I'd thought Astrid needed one simply to be a buffer for an ex. That she was shy and needed a wingman. But that was bullshit. She wasn't really shy. Sure, a buffer had definitely been needed, but everyone here thought she was an ugly duckling. Maybe she'd been one, an awkward teenager. Who the hell wasn't all pimply and weird at fourteen? Looking around, Astrid sure as fuck was a swan. If I was the only one who saw that, fine. We'd be out of here on Sunday.

In the meantime, it was going to be a long night. But I had something to distract me. A reason not to say fuck it and storm out. To keep me from wondering who I should punch first. Something in a pretty shade of green who liked my smiles and melted from my kisses.

10

STRID

AFTER THREE HOURS at the club, we followed Amy and my mother back to the house. Thatcher drove the van since he was sober. I was not.

Well, I wasn't drunk either. I'd taken his advice and avoided the jello shots, but I'd certainly made a dent in the wine. But if there was a line for sobriety, the fact that I'd done karaoke with Amy and her maid of honor, Bea, proved I was just on the wrong side.

I wasn't sure if our rendition of *I Will Survive* was a reminder I'd get through the weekend. But I'd been constantly reminded I wasn't doing it alone. I'd frequently looked for Thatcher. When I wasn't looking for him, I wanted him. Because... yeah, he was gorgeous, and he was mine for the weekend.

It was obvious the difference bringing him made on my fun. I'd been included. Amy forgot I was fat or a lowly baker. My mother must have recognized Thatcher was a better catch than Franklin Pierce. Whatever their reason... I hadn't cared. I'd had fun.

I'd *actually* had fun.

Again, the wine had helped.

Thatcher's winks from across the room sure as shit made me feel wanted. Like I belonged to someone. That we were *together*. He made me feel wanted. Desirable.

Sexy.

"Astrid, dear. I'm sure Thatcher will want to stay in the guest room since your bed is so small," Mother said, setting her purse and keys on the round table in the center of the entry. It was two stories, with marble on the floor and two staircases on the left and right that curved to the second floor central hallway in the middle. It was a little much, but I was used to it. I had no idea what Thatcher thought of my parents' house. Mansion, really. But since Cutthroat was known for being the winter playground of the rich and famous, I didn't think he was surprised.

"It's a queen," I countered. "I gave up my childhood twin size in eleventh grade."

She looked me over. Ah. Even in my wine fog, I understood.

And I'd thought for a few hours that my family would be normal instead of petty. Stupid me.

"Don't worry, Patricia, we don't need a big bed." Thatcher wrapped his arm around my waist, pulled me close. "I like Astrid close. *Real* close."

As the evening wore on, my desire to be truly together with him grew. I liked him. He was nice. Friendly. He hadn't run off for the Manning Ranch when I'd been in the ladies room.

He was here.

And when I said my desire to be truly together with him grew, I also meant more than just in the same room. I wanted to be with him. I desired him. The looks, the winks, the smiles... it was all foreplay.

It had started with the kiss. I hadn't wanted it to stop, but I wasn't into exhibitionism. But as we drove through the dark night, I thought of his mouth on mine. The way he'd held me. Tipped me back. Licked into me. One of his hands had been on the back of my head, the other cupping my ass.

He knew how big my ass was. And I knew how big his dick was. I hadn't held it, but I'd felt that hard length between us. Not just earlier, but in his office the weekend before.

I wanted him. I wanted that fling Mary had mentioned.

Especially now that he'd just alluded to sharing a bed with me to my mother. Her mouth hung open... again, by his response.

"Right, sweets?" he asked, running a thumb over my lower lip, his pale eyes watching the motion.

I blinked, then licked the tip of his thumb. "Thatcher's staying with me."

Since I was watching him, I saw the way his eyes flared with heat. Darkened.

"Goodnight, Mother. Amy," I said, taking Thatcher's hand and leading him upstairs.

As we ascended, I heard Amy's voice. "How does she get to spend the night with a guy and I can't be with Michael tonight?"

"Because your dress is white for a reason. Hers is gray."

Thatcher squeezed my fingers at the insinuation. I wasn't a virgin and Mother thought Amy was.

I went down the corridor and pulled Thatcher into my room, then shut the door behind us.

He glanced around, took in the pale blue walls, the cream carpet. During the day, the windows overlooked Cutthroat Mountain, but he only had eyes for me.

"No boy band posters?"

"My mother redecorated when I went to college. The walls used to be green and yes, there were boy band posters. I'm not telling you which."

Going over to the bed, he took off his hat, tossed it

aside and winked. "It'd be weird to sleep in here with you with Justin Timberlake eyeing us." He bounced up and down.

The bed squeaked. He did it again. And again.

"What are you doing?"

"If your mother thinks you're a hymen-free hussy, then she might as well hear a show."

I burst out laughing.

He put his finger to his lips and grinned. "Shh."

I heard the clack of high heels out, then silence. Amy's room and the master suite were further down the hall. They could definitely hear. And wonder, although the sound made it pretty obvious.

Oh. My. God.

I walked over to Thatcher, stood between his parted knees as he continued to bounce up and down. "You don't care what they think?" I asked. "They barely know you and this isn't the best impression."

"They think what they want no matter what we do," he replied, his voice tipped low.

That was so true. They judged everyone regardless of the truth or wanting to know it.

"As for a good impression—" he continued with a wink, "—they'll think I've got great stamina in the sack. If you moan a little, they'll also think I'm very skilled."

"You are crazy," I whispered back, trying not to smile.

But I wanted Thatcher. I wanted to *really* make the bed squeak. I wanted his hands on me. His mouth.

Maybe it was the wine. Maybe I was crazy. Hell, maybe I was more myself than I'd ever been. But Thatcher was sitting so close he could lean forward and suck my nipple into his mouth. Six feet plus of ginger hotness. I wanted to run my fingers through that red hair, feel the rasp of his whiskers against my palm. Hell, against the insides of my thighs.

I didn't think, only acted.

"I... I have dirty thoughts about you," I said as I undid the thin belt at my waist, let it fall to the floor.

Thatcher stopped moving and started watching. He wasn't saying no. He wasn't saying anything at all. Except his eyes held the heat and desire that made me bold.

I grabbed the hem of my dress, lifted it up an inch at a time, then worked it over my head and tossed it aside. I wasn't going to get up in the morning and have my mother look at me as if I was going to hell without doing any of the things that were going to get me there.

I wanted orgasms and Thatcher was going to give them to me. And he was just catching on to that fact.

11

HATCHER

HOLY SHIT. Astrid in green satin bra and panties, and *only* bra and panties, was the prettiest thing I'd ever seen. Screw a Montana summer storm. Forget my finished barn house. Who cared about my bar on a crowded summer night? I imagined her prettier than a sunset in Cozumel.

I was in big trouble here. My dick wanted out of my jeans and in her. Now.

All the blood was traveling from my brain south and I was running out of time to talk and make sense.

My fingers itched to reach out and grab, cup, stroke, and caress.

"Sweets, what are you doing?"

The bold smile on her face slipped and so did her confidence right along with it.

Fuck.

"I… thought—"

"You've had a lot of wine."

She nodded and tried to step back. That was when I hooked a hand about her waist and kept her from moving away. Her skin was silky soft and warm. We had to talk fast.

"I'm not drunk. I know what I'm doing," she countered.

"What are you doing?"

She sighed and her shoulders drooped. "I thought I was being seductive, but I can see I've done a horrible job. I'm sorry. I must have gotten the wrong idea."

"Oh, no. Don't for a second doubt yourself. You sure as shit are seductive." I proved this by sliding my hand around and cupping her ass. The one cheek didn't fit in my palm and it was lush, squeezable and definitely spankable.

"Then why did you question me? I mean, most guys would be balls deep by now."

If she only knew. I was separated from *most guys* by the slimmest of margins.

"I'm not fucking you if you might have any kinds of second thoughts in the morning because of too much wine."

"You own a bar," she countered.

I couldn't help it. I grabbed her other ass cheek with my free hand. Oh yeah. Perfection. Soft skin, slick satin.

"Yes."

"Then you can probably tell if someone's too drunk to think clearly. I'm not saying I should be driving a car, but I'm not that impaired."

"True."

"And what gives you the right to question my mind about what I want? If I want you, if I want to ride your dick like a cowgirl at a rodeo, then you should have a say about your consent, not mine."

Shit. She had a point. I was just like her family, questioning her mind. She wasn't stupid. And she wasn't drunk. *That* I could tell. If she had a buzz going, and her dress on the floor had definitely given her some liquid courage, that was okay.

It was me who was stalling. I wanted Astrid. Too much. My dick was wondering why it wasn't balls deep like she'd mentioned. But my head was involved. Obviously, since we were *talking* and not fucking.

That meant I cared a little too much. If she was just a random woman from the bar who I fucked in my office, then I wouldn't have thought twice.

This was *Astrid.* In emerald satin.

Not only was I going to get fucked, but I was truly fucked as well, because this fake boyfriend shit was not going as planned. But my dick was waiting. And so was Astrid.

"You're right," I admitted. "You want to ride my dick like a cowgirl at a rodeo?"

She had the boots on to prove it.

She blushed, bit her lip and nodded.

"Then you will. Got any other fantasies?"

She pushed her glasses up. "I think one's all I'm brave enough to share tonight."

My fingers curled into the top of her panties and slowly slid them down her hips. I held her eyes as I spoke. "I've got a few. But ladies first."

Her hands stopped mine. "My fantasy has you naked."

I grinned up at her. "Yes, ma'am." I lifted my hands from her so she could step back to give me room to rise and strip.

As I should have done all along, I stopped thinking and got busy. I was down to my boxers when I thought again.

Shit.

"I don't have protection. We can play, but riding my dick's out."

Her eyes were on my body, not my face. I should have felt objectified, but it was tit for tat. Or tit for dick.

She shook her head and picked up the gift bag she'd been given at the party. Dumping it onto the bed, I looked at the contents.

"Bachelorette party favors," she explained.

Pink dildo still in packaging.

Fur lined handcuffs.

A long string of condoms.

A small bottle of lube.

A butt plug with a green gem on the base.

I was catching on that Astrid liked green. And seeing that color sparkling between parted ass cheeks?

Fuck. Me.

I stared at the haul wide-eyed. And my dick got impossibly harder just thinking about using these things with Astrid. "Jesus, what the hell do ladies usually do at bachelorette parties?"

She shrugged. "I've been to one other and we went out to lunch and got pedicures. The favor bag had scented lotion, an eye mask, and cute flip flops in it. I assume the maid of honor, Bea, bought all this. Gag gift or maybe she wanted the stuff and needed the favor bag excuse to get the stuff for herself. Who knows?" She grabbed the condoms and they dangled from her fingers. "Will this do?"

I snatched them, tossed the rest of the things back in the bag and set it on the side table. "Let's find out."

Tugging down my boxers, my dick bounced free.

"Shit," she whispered.

I looked to her. "What?"

"That dick is *not* fake."

Gripping the base, I gave it one long pump. "Every eight inches is real, sweets."

Knowing I wasn't going to have many brain cells left, I ripped off a condom from the strip and rolled it on. Then I climbed onto her bed, adjusted the pillow behind my head.

All the while, she stood there and watched.

"Your turn, sweets. I've got a thing for your tits. Show them to me."

She blushed, but in a good way. I hoped the way I was looking at her, the way my dick was pointing straight at the ceiling that she knew I was into her. So fucking into her.

With a flick of her fingers at the front clasp, the bra parted and her tits bounced free.

"Fucking gorgeous," I said when she let the garment fall to the floor. "Panties off and get over here."

She shimmied her panties down her legs.

"Leave the boots."

Yeah, I was being bossy as fuck, but if she wanted to ride my dick, then I wanted those cowgirl boots on as she did it.

After she kicked her panties to the side, she stood back up, her tits swaying with the motion.

Every inch of her was perfect. And that pussy... a little patch of dark hair capped pink lips that glistened with her need. I could see her clit all hard and ready to play. I licked my lips, eager to get my mouth on her, but I could wait. Later.

Now, I crooked my finger and she came over, crawled up and straddled me. I couldn't resist reaching up and cupping her breasts. Her dark hair brushed the backs of my hands. "Thatcher," she whispered, her head falling back. She was sensitive and I wondered if I could get her to come just like this. I could spend all night trying.

"These... fuck, sweets. I'm obsessed with them. Lean forward. I've gotta get them in my mouth."

She leaned forward and one nipple hovered over my lips. I lifted my head, sucked the pink tip into my mouth.

A moan slipped from her lips as I felt the tip harden against my tongue.

Perfection. I alternated between the two full globes, ready to die a happy man.

"God, that feels so good."

I let her go with a pop and she looked down at me. She flicked her hair back, then took her glasses off. I took them from her, reached out and set them on the side table beside the favor bag.

"You wet for me?"

I knew she was. I could feel it on my thighs.

"So wet," she whispered.

"Rise up. Take me in you."

She lifted up, slowly lowered herself so I was positioned at her entrance. She gripped the base and I hissed, but watched her as she lowered down. One fucking slow inch at a time.

"Fuck," I growled, trying not to thrust up and fill her too fast.

Slowly she sank down until she sat upon my thighs. Her inner walls rippled as she adjusted to me.

I waited with my teeth gritted together. Finally, she blinked, set her hands on my chest.

"Go for it, cowgirl," I told her.

She smiled then. Yeah, she fucking smiled. She was crammed full with my dick and she looked at me as if this was fun. Which it was, but with her hair covering part of her face and her tits sticking out and just... fuck.

I was in trouble here.

When she started to move, I was a goner. She used her hands to brace herself, but she rode me, slow at first, then faster, following her pleasure. I watched her. The way her tits swayed and bounced, her perfect ass slapped against my thighs. Her inner walls practically milked the cum from my balls.

I wasn't going to last, and I usually lasted a hell of a lot longer than this. But she was too perfect. Too real. I licked the pad of my thumb, then reached between us and found that hard pearl and circled it.

Her eyes met mine, flared wide and then went blurry. She came on a low moan, her head tipping back so her hair tickled my thighs. Her pussy clenched down and practically strangled my dick as she came.

I couldn't hold off a second longer, just grabbed her hips, lifted her up, dropped her down hard. Once, twice. Then I spurted hot and thick. Long as fuck. I went blind. Lost brain cells. The world could explode, and I'd never know, but I had, because as I came back to myself, I realized the woman sprawled across my chest had changed me.

The one thing I knew, that sure as fuck hadn't been fake.

 STRID

I WOKE UP, as usual, at four. At first, I was completely confused where I was, then had a moment of panic when I felt the arm over my waist and cupping my breast. It all came back in a flash. My parents' house. The wedding. Thatcher. Thatcher's thorough obsession with my boobs. Even in his sleep, he was touching one.

Dawn was approaching, but there wasn't yet a hint of pink in the sky. Only the early start of the birds chirping indicated I wasn't late waking up. Except I didn't have to bake. I wasn't even in The Bend.

But I *was* wide awake. Not only because I'd trained

myself to get up at this ridiculous hour, but because I was in bed with Thatcher Manning.

Naked.

I'd kicked off my cowgirl boots when he'd gone to the bathroom to ditch the condom. Then he'd pulled me into his arms and I remembered nothing after.

His dick was pressed against my lower back and even unconscious, the guy sported wood. Carefully, I slid from the bed and slipped on Thatcher's shirt and snapped it closed on the way to the kitchen. I dug through the fridge for something to eat, but my mother didn't cook, and they didn't consider leftovers an option. Amy only ate salads and drank smoothies so there wasn't even an egg to scramble.

I shut the fridge door and stifled a scream. Thatcher stood there, arms crossed over his bare chest. He was only in his boxers. His hair was a mess—thanks to me. I'd flipped on the undercabinet lights when I'd come in so the room was lit, but not brightly. Every hard plane of Thatcher's chiseled body stood out in relief. The six-pack abs. The sturdy thighs. The thick bulge in his boxers.

"Sweets, what the hell are you doing up?" His voice was raspy from sleep and his whiskers were dark.

After what we'd done earlier, I didn't hesitate to run my fingers over them to discover they were soft, but raspy.

"This is when I usually wake up."

His gaze dipped to his shirt. "Looks better on you."

I didn't know what to say to that, but I liked wearing his shirt. And nothing else.

"I've got something we can do to pass the time. You game?"

Was I game for more sex with Thatcher? Um, yeah.

"You got your fantasy earlier," he murmured. "My turn?"

I licked my lips at the possibilities. I knew Thatcher liked my body. He'd liked it when I was on top. But beyond that...

"Your turn," I whispered, my hand pressing against his chest and then sliding down. Lower and lower still.

"You good with me taking control?" he asked.

Amy and my parents were asleep in their rooms. They could come down at any time, although I couldn't imagine them waking at this time of night. Or morning.

"Sure."

"Good girl. Then bend over the counter."

My eyes flared, then flicked to the huge center island. This was his fantasy? Here?

He must have sensed my concern because he asked, "Think I'd do anything to hurt you? That all I want to do is get you to come all over my dick?"

He'd seen the people I'd grown up with. He had a pretty good idea of what I'd gone through growing up. One thing I couldn't stand was being humiliated or degraded. Thatcher wouldn't do that to me. A thrill shot through me, and it wasn't panic.

It was need.

I turned and set my palms on the cool granite, then leaned forward.

He didn't wait but nudged my feet wider apart with one of his knees. His hands slid up the backs of my thighs and pushed his shirt up to my waist.

"I love this ass."

"It's big."

"You want me to spank you here in your parents' kitchen?" he asked, keeping his voice low.

The idea of him spanking me made me clench my butt cheeks in anticipation.

"You like that idea."

"Not here."

His hand caressed over my butt. "No, not here."

I heard the sound of a condom wrapper, then a pause where I turned to watch him slide the protection down his length.

He reached around me, gripped the front of his shirt I wore and tugged the snaps open.

My breasts spilled out and he cupped them as he thrust deep.

I moaned, then bit my lip.

"Shh," he murmured in my ear. "You don't want your parents to know you're getting fake fucked by your fake boyfriend."

He took me hard as he played with my breasts, tugged on my nipples. Whispered dirty words. With his other hand, he coiled my hair around his fingers and pulled. Gently, but still. I'd never had it tugged before and it was hot as hell. Especially when it arched my back and he groaned when my breasts thrust out.

I'd never met a guy who was so much of a breast man.

Reaching between us, I rubbed my clit. I needed to come. And now because I was so worked up. It was like I craved Thatcher, craved what he could do with his dick. I could barely move. Between my hips trapped between the granite and Thatcher, my hair snagged... I couldn't do anything but feel. I'd think about how quick I orgasmed with him another time. I just gave over to the feel of him surrounding me, pounding me, taking what he wanted from my body while I came on a whimper, my glasses practically falling off my face.

He followed me, thrusting deep and slapping a hand on the granite by my head.

Our ragged breathing was the only sound in the house.

"Thank you," I finally whispered.

"For what?" he asked, his voice rough as he pulled out. "Fucking you? Sweets, I do that gladly."

"Well, for that too, I guess. I'll never think of this kitchen in the same way again."

I felt his smile against my skin. "Same goes for my shirt. Come on, back to bed."

Later, when we woke up for the softball game, I didn't panic when I thought about being late. I had an answer planned for my sister. But it was long and hard, and I *really* didn't want to share.

 HATCHER

SHE PANICKED because we were late, fidgeting in the van as she pointed the way to the high school ball fields. She was in running shorts which showed off her legs in ways I hadn't seen before and a bakery t-shirt. Of course, I envisioned her tits in all their bare glory. Her hair was pulled back in a long ponytail. And that made me remember how I'd gripped it in the middle of the night. I hadn't expected to fuck her over the kitchen counter, but it wasn't something I would forget. Ever. Taking her so roughly, so carnally. And it had all been fake.

Right. We may have been calling everything we'd

been doing fake, but my dick was the smart one and knew that the hot clamp of her pussy when she'd come had been anything but pretend.

"There they are." She pointed, although it was obvious where we were going since there were two fields, one of them empty.

I pulled into a spot between a Cutthroat police SUV and a six-figure convertible that only came out to play for about three months a year.

Before she hopped out, I grabbed her arm. She looked over her shoulder at me, surprised. "Do I need to give you another fake orgasm so you're relaxed?"

She blushed, pushed her glasses up. "Seventh inning stretch?" A sly smile spread across her face when I had to adjust myself.

She hopped out and I met her by the hood. Through the chain link fence that separated the playing field from the parking lot, I took in the group.

Astrid's mother, Amy, Michael. Bea. Bunky and Lynn. The former president. Eddie. The wedding planner, Kit, who must have been roped into this. A few others I hadn't met before.

"Can your mother play softball?" I wondered. While Astrid's mom couldn't be more than fifty-five, I figured the only thing she ran to was a shoe sale. She was in black ankle pants and a fuschia blouse. A blouse. To play softball.

"No. But she wouldn't miss this for anything."

"But your dad would?" I didn't see him anywhere.

"Last night there was liquor," she said.

I mentally added *and hookers.*

"I'm sure he's at the hospital. He'll be at the rehearsal dinner tonight. I'm sorry I never asked if you were okay with this."

"Softball?" I shrugged. "What can go wrong?"

I should have known with this crowd, probably a hell of a lot.

We walked onto the field and joined the group by one of the dugouts. Patricia turned to us, her assessing gaze raking over us. "There you are."

"We're here!" Astrid replied brightly.

Michael came over, gave me a head nod. I'd learned the night before he was an accountant and I'd played against his high school football team back in the day. Out of the guys I'd met, he was as decent as Astrid had said. He wore gym shorts and an old college t-shirt, far from the others in their designer athleisure-wear. Bunky was dressed for the links, not right field. Eddie's sneakers cost more than a fancy saddle. I didn't even look at any of the women in their skin-tight leggings and crop tops.

"We've already chosen teams," Michael said. "Amy and I are team captains. You and Astrid are with me, Edward, Bea, Bunky, Kit and her boyfriend, Nix."

I only nodded because being stuck with Eddie and Bunky? Fucking awful.

"Batter up!" Patricia shouted from behind home plate.

I glanced at Michael, who frowned. "She's the umpire."

Astrid came over in a ball cap, the words "Groom's Team" embroidered on the front. She handed one to me, another to Michael. "Here."

I looked at it, sighed, and put it on. I'd left my Stetson in Astrid's room.

"Hey, I'm Nix Knight." We shook hands. "I know your brother, Huck."

"Oh?"

"The police SUV's mine. I'm a Cutthroat detective and I've worked with Huck on a case or two. My girl, Kit, asked me to come to even out the teams."

Michael handed me a glove and pushed me toward left field. "Nice to meet you," I called to Nix as he cut to first base.

Since there weren't enough players to round out full teams, I stayed in close and was expected to be a mix of outfield, shortstop and third base.

Amy was up first, followed by four others. They made it as far as second base before they had three outs. Astrid, as catcher, easily caught a fly ball to finish off the top of the inning. Either they were all hungover from the party the night before or they just sucked.

Bunky joined me as I walked back to the dugout. "Surprised to see you here, Manning," he said.

"Why, Bunky? After what Charles said, I thought you'd be at the casino today."

He hated that nickname when he was in The Bend. I had to assume he went by Thomas here in Cutthroat.

"I figured you more for a guy looking for a hot piece of ass instead of a hot bank account," he replied. "Maybe I was wrong about you."

The only guy who could think of Astrid as a hot piece of ass was me. While Bunky's words were meant to rile me, I only saw them as an attack on Astrid.

"Your nose is looking better. What did you tell Lynn happened last weekend?" I raised my hand and waved in his wife's direction even though she wasn't looking our way.

Sawyer had punched him in the nose when he'd learned Bunky was the ex who'd lied to Kelsey about being married, and about being in love with her.

His jaw clenched as if he could crack the back molars and his cheeks flushed. He grabbed a bat and stormed off, which was great because now he was out of my face.

Astrid came into the dugout and sat her borrowed glove on the bench then grabbed a bottle of water from the cooler. She eyed me but didn't approach. She knew I had a beef with Bunky.

Michael bat first, got a double and kissed Amy who was playing second base.

Bunky was up next.

"You good?" I asked Astrid.

She gave me a quick smile, left the dugout with a bat and said over her shoulder. "Oh yeah. I got this."

She was on deck and I missed Bunky strike out because of her swinging a bat for warmup. Her t-shirt went taut over her tits when she swung. I'd sucked on those luscious globes. Cupped them. Watched them sway as we fucked.

I had to look away because my shorts didn't hide a hard on.

Fortunately, Bunky stomped back to the dugout, which was the best thing to make my dick go down. He swore to himself as Astrid settled in behind home plate to wait for the pitch. Did she even play softball? Had she played sports as a kid? I didn't see her as big on field hockey or ballet. Too frou frou for her. I figured—

Holy shit. She launched that ball into outer space on the first swing. It easily cleared the fence.

I watched as she ran the bases, a perfect soft smile on her face as she did. Michael ran home and waited for her to follow, then gave her a high five. The rest of us on the team came out of the dugout to join him, gave her high fives as well.

I gave her one plus a fake kiss. A really fucking good one. "I think I'm going to call you Slugger from now on."

She grinned and it wasn't fake at all. "Softball scholarship to USC."

"Impressive," I said, taking her hand and sitting beside her in the dugout.

Eddie followed her and struck out. I went after, hit a line drive and got a single. Another bridesmaid who introduced herself as Tara, followed, but also struck out.

It became very clear who had played ball before.

After collecting our mitts, we headed back to the outfield. Eddie caught up to me.

"You missed the real bachelor party last night."

"Oh?"

Watching Astrid straddling me and taking my dick for a ride was better than seeing any strip show a hooker could offer.

"Three strippers. They were incredible." Eddie cupped his hands in front of his chest. "Sandra, the one with the big titties and the bare pussy did things that had to be illegal."

"Huh," I added, taking off my Groom's Team hat and wiping my forehead.

"I mean, a girlfriend's fine and all, but will they suck your dick like a Hoover? Astrid never—"

I held up my hand. "Don't finish that sentence," I warned.

He smiled at me. "Come on, you know Astrid like I do. She'll never get down and dirty like any of those strippers. You need to think of the Sandras out there in order to get off when she's beneath you."

That was it. There on the Cutthroat High School softball field, I lost my shit. I didn't give a fuck if someone trash talked me. Hell, I heard it all the time from drunks at the bar.

But no one... *no one,* bad mouthed Astrid.

I pushed him in the arm, which knocked him off balance. His mitt fell to the grass.

"What the fuck?"

I narrowed my eyes. Snarled. "I said to shut the fuck up."

"You're only between her thighs for her money. Trust me, a frigid pussy's a hefty price for a bank account like hers."

I punched him. Like Astrid and her home run, I only needed one swing. His nose crunched beneath my knuckles and I felt a thrill of satisfaction when blood spurted. He grabbed his nose and bent at the waist.

"Dude, what the fuck?" Eddie shouted. Blood slid down his face, dripped off his chin.

I stood there, fists clenched, practically daring him to say more.

"Whoa, what's going on here?" Michael asked. He put his arms out as if he were a ref separating two rowdy hockey players. I took a step back, then another.

"He shared some things that were better off left unsaid," I replied, trying to be diplomatic.

Astrid came over, stood beside me. She went up on

her tiptoes, whispered in my ear. "I've wanted to do that for years."

I looked down at her, took in those green eyes behind her glasses. The mischief in them. "Yeah, it felt damned good," I whispered back.

Amy ran up, got in Eddie's face.

"You told him?" Amy waved her arms, eyes wild. Eddie could barely see her around his hand. Blood was staining his fucking golf shirt. "How could you tell him?"

Everyone came over, circled around so we were all in the middle of the outfield.

"Tell him what?" Eddie asked her, playing dumb.

"Do you know what she's talking about?" Astrid murmured.

Eddie wasn't in a relationship with anyone as far as I knew, or at least not anyone who'd been invited to the wedding festivities. He could fuck Sandra the Hooker until his dick fell off from an STD for all I cared, but I doubted he wanted to share that with the group.

I had no idea what Amy was talking about, nor why she was freaking out.

"That broken nose says you did," Amy went on. "I can't believe you."

"No idea," I replied to Astrid. We were low-talking so we didn't interrupt the soap opera in front of us. My money was on Amy.

"I assume you punched him in the nose for a reason," Astrid murmured.

"Oh yeah."

"And Amy knows why?"

I shrugged, unsure.

"Amy, this isn't the right—" She spun on Michael, who'd taken hold of her arm.

"Everyone wants to ruin this weekend for me. Especially Astrid," she snarled, like a feral cat.

I bristled and out of the corner of my eye, I saw Astrid did too. I laced my fingers with hers.

"She makes a sub-par wedding cake, then she brings a boyfriend that everyone's talking about instead of me. This fight... " She waved her hand between Eddie and Astrid. "I told you it had to stay a secret. It's not my fault you told Thatcher, Edward. Now Astrid knows."

"Yeah, I know everything," Astrid said, straight-faced.

She had no fucking clue, but she was playing Amy for details.

But it was Patricia who gave it up. "Amy, it's not your fault Astrid couldn't keep Edward's interest. Edward sleeping with you on the side was her fault. She practically drove you into his arms."

Say what?

Astrid's fingers squeezed mine. Amy was the woman Eddie had cheated with behind Astrid's back?

"Jesus, this was years ago," Michael said. "We hadn't even met yet."

Michael was fine with whatever sex Amy'd had before they met, even if it meant she'd been the "other woman." Even if she'd done something so cruel to her own sister. That was completely fucked up. Maybe he was like this because he'd enjoyed Sandra the Hooker the night before. If so, he wasn't one to throw stones.

Hell, everyone we'd met in Cutthroat, except maybe Kit and Donovan, was insane.

"Amy," Astrid said.

Amy whipped around and glared at Astrid. Her chest was heaving. "What?"

"I'm done. You got your free cake. You got your man." She pointed at Eddie, then Michael. "And your man. I'm leaving. You didn't want me here anyway. But I'm sure as shit not sharing Thatcher."

Astrid spun to face her mother. "You put my ex as best man in a wedding when you knew he fucked me over with the bride. You chose *Eddie* over me. My van's a shame to you. My clothing is. My ability to see disappoints you. I'm out. Done. You know where I live. You know what I am. Show up or not. I don't give a shit any longer. You can take that stupid *gray* dress and fuck off."

Amy and Patricia had the same look on their faces. They weren't taking her words to heart, they were just stunned that she stood up for herself. Told them to fuck off.

That was my girl. I couldn't have been more proud of her. She swung and hit it right out of the fucking park.

"Keys," Astrid said. "Thatcher, give me the keys to my van."

She'd called them on their shit. Yet I knew they weren't going to change.

"Now."

I did, after pulling them from my shorts' pocket.

Snatching them, she took off, heading across the field toward the parking lot, dropping her ball cap in the grass on the way. I looked at the group. At Michael for being prepared to marry a woman like Amy. At Patricia for being the worst mother ever. At Eddie, who was going to have a busted nose and two black eyes as best man tomorrow. Then at Amy, who was Queen Bitch.

I didn't say a word, Astrid had said enough, only just jogged to catch up to her. Because the one thing that wasn't fake was how I felt right now.

"Wait up!" I called.

She didn't stop, not until she got to the van and fumbled with getting the key in the lock.

"Astrid. Let me drive. You're in no condition to—"

She spun on me, her ponytail whipping around. "I can drive when I'm upset, Thatcher."

I held up my hands. "Yeah, I know, but you don't have to."

Tears filled her eyes and she pushed at her glasses.

Oh shit. Not tears. This was the first time I'd seen her break down, even after everything she'd been through. The passive aggressiveness. The accusations. The belittling. She didn't even know the half of the things I'd heard. What her father had said about her. What Eddie had said. Bunky, too. I wanted to take her to the ranch and tuck her into my farmhouse and shield her from the world. To tell her every day how perfect she was, just the way she was. She didn't need any of the losers here in Cutthroat. She didn't need her parents or sister.

She blinked, then set her hands on her hips. "Yeah, I do."

"I'm here," I replied. She'd let me help her before.

"No, you're not."

I frowned. She wasn't making sense. "Sweets, I'm standing right here."

"You're not really *with* me," she added. "You're my fake boyfriend, remember?"

I rolled my eyes, flung a hand in the air. "Come on, we're past that, don't you think?"

I wanted to pull her into my arms, hug the shit out of her. She didn't get enough of them in her life, and I wanted to be the one to change that. It was different than sex. Different than my obsession with her body. I wanted her, to comfort her. To make all her problems in life go away. I was working on it one broken nose at a time.

She shifted and crossed her arms. "You're going to Mexico, remember? You don't want a relationship."

Shit.

It was my turn to be scolded. My own words were being tossed at me and I didn't like the feel of it. Mexico didn't sound so exotic right about now. The warm sun, the beach, and the ocean, all of that wasn't really going to keep me warm over the winter months. But Astrid could.

For the first time, I could see why Huck wanted to hunker down with Sarah. Stay home. *Nap.* Make babies.

But I'd avoided all that in my life because *things happened.* Kelsey almost died in a fucking fire last weekend. Sarah and Huck were ripped apart for six years. Turned out, they'd even lost a baby. Our parents had died. Shit happened and that hurt. Going to Mexico was a way to ensure the love trap that my brothers were falling into didn't happen to me.

"So you're what? Pushing me away because of something Amy and Eddie did?"

She looked away. When she caught sight of the shit show still out on the field, she had her answer. "Yeah. I'm pushing you away. Not because of Amy. I'm pushing you away because I never had you. I can take care of myself because those people—" She pointed to the group. "—don't give a shit about me. I've known that for years. That's why I left. Why I stayed away. I thought maybe things would be different this time. A wedding's a happy occasion. Maybe they'd be different. If I brought a boyfriend, they'd see me differently. But no."

"Screw them," I said. "But not me."

"I already did," she countered, her words almost cruel. They made what we'd done the night before seem like I was a paid hooker. I was the Sandra for her. "We're done, Thatcher. Obviously, I'm not going to the wedding tomorrow. Your services are no longer needed."

"My *services?* I'm not talking about that. And you'll remember you liked those *services* just as much as me," I snapped right back. I ripped off the hat to run my hand over my head, realized it was the fucking ball cap and not my Stetson, and tossed it aside.

"Fine. I loved it. But it was a fling. Meaningless. You knew it. I knew it. It's better to walk away now."

"You don't want to try, whatever this is between us?"

What was I saying? I couldn't keep her, but I didn't want to let her go.

"Do you? Because you were just as clear as me. I'm not the one leaving the country."

She pointed to the dugouts where everyone was

collecting their stuff. Softball wasn't going to happen now. "Besides, I'm not turning into that. You saw it first-hand what love is like. It's not real. It's a lie. I'm sparing you—both of us—now."

I thought of Claire's words. How love was easy.

No way. But this was the closest I'd ever felt to a woman and it had all been pretend. If it was real, I'd be gutted. Exactly the reason I'd avoided it.

Still, someone like her deserved to be loved. To show up a guy with her killer softball skills. With her amazing baking. With her need for promptness. Hell, for her need for someone to make her first. Above everything and everyone else.

And I couldn't give her that.

Because right now, it fucking hurt and we'd been faking it all along. If it were real, I wasn't going to survive and I'd been in survival mode since I was twelve.

"What about last night?" I asked.

The question made me sound like a total girl.

She swiped at the tears streaming down her cheeks. "Like I told you then. You're dick wasn't fake."

Her attention went to getting the key in the lock. She got the door open and was inside before I could even think of anything more. I watched as she backed out of the spot and gunned it out of the parking lot.

HATCHER

"Need a ride?" I hadn't realized I'd been staring at the main road until Nix spoke.

I turned, ran a hand over my head. "Yeah, thanks. Looks like I'm stuck in Cutthroat."

"Think she'll come back for you when she's feeling better?"

I laughed. "I don't think she's coming back. Ever."

Kit joined us. She offered me a sad smile. "That was... interesting."

"Wedding still on?" I asked.

She rolled her eyes. "As an event planner, it sounds

pretty sad, but if I got paid by a marriage's success, I'd be out of business."

Nix wrapped an arm around her waist, kissed the top of her head.

"I'm going to give Thatcher a ride back to The Bend."

She nodded. "I'll tell Donovan, but I'll be at the rehearsal dinner tonight."

Twenty minutes later, we'd picked up our things from Astrid's bedroom in her parents' house—let in by a housekeeper—and on the road toward The Bend in Nix's police SUV. It was pretty much identical to Huck's so I was familiar with all the buttons and gadgets.

"That is one fucked up family," Nix finally said. "And I've seen some shit."

"Yeah."

"I'm guessing you learned about Edward and Amy right before you punched him in the nose."

I looked out the window at the passing prairie. "I punched Eddie because he deserved it. The fucker," I grumbled. "I didn't know it was Amy he'd cheated with until she fucked up and let her paranoia get the best of her. I guess Astrid leaving town all those years ago made it easy to keep the secret."

"I can't believe Michael's cool with that shit and made Edward the best man."

I shrugged. "I missed the after-hours bachelor party, but based on what Astrid's dad told me about hookers, Michael probably isn't all that concerned about fidelity."

"Yeah, I heard about the hookers." I glanced at him, but he didn't take his eyes off the road. "Comes with the job."

"I don't think any of them give a shit about monogamy, for that matter. I know for a fact that Bunky's a fucking cheater."

He glanced my way, arched a dark brow. "Bunky?"

"Thomas Bunker."

"Ah. The slimy guy on our team?"

"That doesn't narrow it down much, but yeah. He's from The Bend. Sadly, my brothers and I grew up with him."

"Small world," he commented. "It's a good thing Astrid's got you. Shitty relationships might be everywhere, but when you find a good one, you keep her."

"Kit?" I asked, hoping to steer the conversation away from me.

He smiled. "Yeah. Donovan and I are lucky."

I didn't know who Donovan was, but I'd heard that some guys in Cutthroat shared a woman. Based on the other relationships I'd seen in that town, maybe there was something to be said for it.

I kept my mouth shut because I couldn't even make a fake relationship work.

But if it was so fake, why did I feel like shit?

———

ASTRID

"W<small>HAT THE</small>—" Mary said, putting the frosting she'd just mixed into the walk-in fridge. She shut the door behind her and eyed me. "Say that again."

"It was Amy," I repeated. "Edward cheated on me with my sister."

She stared. "Holy shit. I'm calling your aunt." She went for the phone, picked up the tin we put broken, unsellable cookies in, and handed it to me.

I dropped onto my stool with the tin and pulled out a piece of a snickerdoodle. I heard Mary talking but didn't pay her any attention. In fact, I didn't remember driving back from Cutthroat. I'd stared at the road and drove on autopilot as I thought about my fucked-up family. My life. Thatcher.

Aunt Jean must have been at the library because she came through the door within minutes. She wore black pants with a plain white blouse, but over it she had on a pale blue t-shirt that read *Five out of four people have problems with fractions.*

I'd seen that one before, which I thought was hilarious. On a normal day.

Today, I wondered if five out of four people had

crazy families or whose sister fucked her boyfriend behind her back.

I watched from the stool as she shooed a straggler who was drinking an iced coffee and reading a book out the door and turned the open sign to closed.

I should have cared that she shut down my business early, or that she was able to do it with such finesse that the guy thought he was doing her a favor instead of the other way around, but I didn't have it in me. The store closed early on Saturdays so I'd probably only miss a few late stragglers.

"Upstairs," she ordered when she took one look at me. "Bring the tin."

She didn't wait, only started up the back steps to my apartment above the store. The arrangement suited me well, especially since I had to be up so early. It was a short commute and great in the winter.

I followed, Mary taking up the rear. Aunt Jean was already on my small couch.

"Mary said you were back early," Aunt Jean said. "For a second I thought maybe you couldn't stay away from the shop, but then I remembered who you were related to."

"Edward cheated on me with Amy." I said it like I was ripping off a Band-Aid.

Her lips thinned, but she didn't even blink. "That is not surprising."

"You knew?" I shrieked, waving my arms around.

"Astrid, sit down," she replied calmly.

When I flopped onto the other end of the couch, she took my hand. Mary settled into my overstuffed armchair, the one I snuggled into to read.

"I didn't know," Aunt Jean began. "But with our family, is it really all that surprising?"

I paused, clutching my fingers together in my lap. "Amy is a total bitch. I hate using that word because it's so gender specific, but she is. But this? It's..."

"Do you really want Edward?" she asked, her eyes a little concerned.

My eyes widened in horror. "Hell no," I replied.

The relief on her face was visible. Clearly she didn't want me with that guy. "Then it doesn't really matter. Even though it was years ago, she did you a favor."

I opened my mouth to argue, then shut it. Maybe she did. If I hadn't heard through the Cutthroat grapevine Edward had cheated in the first place, I'd never have dumped him. I'd like to think I'd have come to my senses about him on my own, but maybe not. I just had to wonder how the gossip hadn't included that it had been Amy. I'd never asked him who it was. It hadn't mattered. Maybe it still didn't when it came to him, but Amy? I wasn't sure if I'd ever get over what she'd done.

Aunt Jean seemed to think it still didn't matter.

I'd left Cutthroat because of the breakup.

"I wouldn't have come here and opened my shop."

"That's right. I'm the only sane one in the family. I've loved having you close and it took a little while, but you've found your place here. You run a successful business. *You* are a success, Astrid, no matter what your parents or sister say."

"Here, here," Mary said, waving a broken oatmeal raisin then taking a bite. "You wouldn't have me as a best friend either. I should send Amy a thank you card."

I stared at her, then burst out laughing. Then burst into tears.

"Amy's not worth crying over," Aunt Jean said, her voice softer.

"I'm not crying over her," I said, each word coming out in a gaspy sob.

"It's not the dress they're making you wear, is it?" Mary asked.

I shook my head. "I never even tried it on."

"Then what?" Aunt Jean asked, then said, "Oh. It's Thatcher, isn't it?"

I cried and nodded, ate a cookie piece and cried some more. Thatcher was... God, he was perfect. Nice. Charming. Protective. Definitely possessive, especially of my boobs. He dealt with my family like a champ. Fucked me like I was a princess and a slut, and I'd loved every minute of being with him. And then I pushed him away because I felt too much. Instead of running into his arms as he'd offered, I'd done the opposite. Now I was eating broken cookies and crying over a broken heart.

"I... I left him in Cutthroat."

"He's a big boy," Aunt Jean said. "He can get himself home. Did he do something?"

I shook my head. "No. I did. I fell in love with him."

———

THATCHER

"Let me get this straight. You went with Astrid Turnbuckle to her sister's wedding as a fake boyfriend."

I nodded at Alice, who was sitting at the foot of the huge kitchen table. She'd sent Claire down to my barn house to retrieve me for dinner. I might be thirty years old but I knew it was something I couldn't refuse, no matter how I felt.

Huck and Claire sat facing me, Sarah on my right. Sawyer was working at the firehouse and Kelsey was in town. Alice had made one of my favorites, chicken and dumplings. I hardly tasted it.

When she gave the one sentence recap of the weekend, I swallowed hard, my latest bite stuck in my throat.

"Yes, ma'am," I replied. She gave me the stare that

in the past meant I was in trouble. "It was what she wanted. That was why she bought me at the auction."

"Then you love each other!" Claire cried out, waving her hands around. "That's what happens when you get bought."

Alice covered her mouth with a napkin, clearly trying to hide her smile. Huck slid his hand down Claire's head, who happily forked a piece of strawberry and shoved it in her mouth.

I wasn't so sure about that. Astrid had left me in Cutthroat. I knew where I stood with her. She'd made it very clear how she felt, and it wasn't love.

All she felt for me was fake, fake, fake.

"No woman wants a man to pretend. That's what gets him in trouble in the first place." Alice added a humph to that and stabbed her fork into a cucumber slice.

"Take Sawyer for example and what happened at the preschool with Kelsey," Huck said.

"What happened to Seesaw?" Claire turned her head and looked up at her father.

"Miss Kelsey thought Seesaw was pretending to be something he wasn't and she got mad. *Real* mad," he added.

Meaning she'd kneed him in the balls.

"I wasn't the only one pretending. She *paid* for me to do it." I knew that was a stupid thing to say but the words fell out anyway. I sounded like I was nine and trying to tell my parents it was Huck's fault the cows had black spots painted on them.

"Why?" Alice asked. "Astrid's a lovely woman. Why would she need to buy a date?"

"She's happily single but wanted a guy to go with her to the wedding. Her ex is the best man," I explained. "She wanted a date to be a buffer."

"That makes sense," Sarah said. "I mean, what better way to have confidence than having a handsome man on your arm in front of an ex?"

"Hey!" Huck muttered.

Sarah tilted her chin and gave him a look. "What?"

"Why is Thatcher the handsome one?"

Sarah rolled her eyes and laughed. "Thatcher's a catch. For someone else," she added, to make him feel better. The idiot. I wasn't the Manning who'd been handcuffed to his headboard.

"You were to be her fake boyfriend for the entire weekend?"

I took a sip of water, set my glass down. "Yes."

"A buffer," Alice repeated.

"Yes."

"So you *buffered* even when you weren't with her ex?" Alice gave me another pointed look.

I caught the innuendo and did everything I could not to blush, or to have my dick get hard remembering all the buffering Astrid and I had done.

"Finished?" Huck asked Claire.

She nodded, then looked to Alice. "May I be excused?"

Alice's glare dropped away and she gave Claire a soft smile. "You may."

Claire hopped down from her booster and Huck handed her her plate to carry to the kitchen. The clatter of the dish hitting the counter was followed by her sneakered feet as they dashed off.

"I think it's kind of cute," Sarah admitted.

"You were at the auction," I said to Alice. "Miss Turnbuckle's the one who bought me. Does it make you feel any better that she was in on this whole thing?"

Alice pursed her lips but didn't say anything.

"What are we missing?" Sarah asked. "If Miss Turnbuckle helped, then there's got to be a good reason."

Alice thought, then nodded in quiet agreement. No one doubted Miss Turnbuckle's integrity.

I huffed out a breath. Where the hell did I start? "Her family's psycho." I hopped up from my chair and paced the kitchen. Just talking about them got me riled. "Besides Miss Turnbuckle, of course. She's Astrid's great-aunt. Her parents and sister, Amy, live in Cutthroat. They think she's fat. That she plays at baking. That she should have turned a blind eye to her ex's cheating. That if she was better at pleasing a man, he wouldn't have cheated in the first place."

Sarah stared, her mouth practically hanging open. "I should give their number to my dad."

O'Banyon was an asshole and they'd probably get along like a house on fire. Which reminded me.

I pointed at Huck. "By the way, you should check out Bunky for the preschool fire and whatever other shit he's got going on."

He arched a brow and his fork stopped halfway to his mouth. "Oh?"

"If her family wasn't fun enough, Bunky and Lynn were at the party last night. Astrid's dad said he was surprised that Bunky had pulled himself out of the casino and wondered if he'd won back the money he'd lost. Bunky looked a little green."

Huck thought for a moment, nodded. "He could have paid that idiot to burn the preschool down for the insurance money but did such a bad job that Bunky won't see a dime. That only makes his situation worse, if he's gambled away his inheritance and won't get money to overhaul that building."

"Didn't you say Lynn's car was stolen?" Sarah asked.

"And didn't Kelsey say they met at a casino in Colorado?" I'd forgotten about that until now.

Huck nodded, then set his fork down. "I'll look into it. If this shakes out, he'll see jail time."

"Thatcher, while you're up, cut a few more slices of the bread," Alice said.

I went around the counter, picked up the bread

knife and started slicing the baguette on the cutting board. I couldn't help but smile. "Bunky behind bars? Couldn't happen to a better person."

"Why are you back early then? Isn't the wedding tomorrow?" Alice asked, steering the topic back to where she wanted it.

I tried not to growl as I ruthlessly cut a slice of bread. "Astrid learned something that made her mad. She left Cutthroat. She's not going to the wedding."

"So you're no longer her boyfriend," Alice added.

I glanced up. "I never was her boyfriend."

"That's good since you're going to Mexico."

"That's what I told her," I said, making sure Alice knew I'd been up front with Astrid. But Cozumel felt really far away. The beach sounded hot and sweaty and dealing with tourists every day seemed more like a pain than fun. And Kent was still waiting for me to reply to his text about going early.

I sliced another piece with more effort than necessary.

"She stood up for herself, skipping the wedding," Alice stated. "Her family will know they disappointed her."

I raised the bread knife and swung it around as I spoke. "Disappointed her? Amy slept with her ex!"

Sarah gasped, but didn't say anything.

"Yeah, that's what she found out. Her ex cheated on Astrid with her own sister."

Alice shrugged. "Between you and this ex, she'll have learned what not to look for in a man."

My eyes bugged out at Alice's words. How calm she was. "I am *nothing* like Eddie. He's an asshole. He doesn't give a shit about her."

She didn't usually like us swearing and called us out on it. Why she wasn't now, I wasn't sure.

"And you do?" Alice asked, cocking her head to the side.

"Yes. She's smart and the most talented artist I've ever met. Have you seen her frosting flowers? She's not fat, she's got perfect curves that I—" I cut myself off on that one. "She's a ringer at softball and when she smiles, the entire room lights up."

Sarah looked at Huck. Huck looked at Sarah. Alice smiled.

"But it was all fake. Everything you did together," Alice prodded.

Why was she being so mild? Wasn't she mad for Astrid? How did she not understand?

"Hell no," I countered. "None of it was. Not one kiss. Not—" I ran a hand over the back of my neck, realized I'd almost cut my head off, then dropped the knife. It clattered on the wooden chopping block. "It was easy. Being with her. Liking her. It was... oh fuck. Claire was right."

"Claire?" Huck asked on a laugh.

"She said it was easy."

"What?" Alice asked.

"Love."

Sarah clapped her hands. I stared at Alice, stunned. She smiled, pleased with herself, taking me around in circles until I got where she wanted me to go.

"I don't love her," I said.

"Then why are you strangling that loaf of bread?" Huck asked, amused.

I glanced down, saw that I'd practically squeezed the bread to death. I let it go, then ran my hands over my face.

"I can't do love," I admitted.

"Why not?" Sarah asked, coming into the kitchen to give me a hug. "It's not so bad."

I looked down at her, saw the happiness on her face. Huck had given this to her. Completed her.

"People die, Sarah. They go away."

Her smile slipped and when she lifted her hand to my jaw, tears filled her eyes. "I know."

I looked up at the ceiling, feeling like a total asshat. "Shit, I'm sorry. Of course you know. Bad things happen." Like her losing the baby she and Huck made.

"But good things do too." She looked to Huck. "So many good things. I think I'm qualified to say that the good far outweighs the bad."

I shook my head. "I barely know her."

Sarah's hand on my cheek gave me a little smack. "We're not telling you to go marry the woman."

"What am I supposed to do?" I felt split open. Raw. Panicked. I didn't talk about feelings. I was the easygoing brother. It was safer being happy-go-lucky. The brother that didn't have the weight of the world on his shoulders. But I did.

I felt it now. I wanted to go to Astrid and make her hurt go away. To fill in the void that her family had made.

"Just pass on going to Mexico and take her on a date."

"It's that simple?" Was it really that simple? Was it easy like Claire said?

"What does your heart tell you?" she asked.

I looked to Alice, who gave a little nod.

Huck stayed quiet, which was probably smart.

My heart was telling me Astrid deserved someone to love her unconditionally. Who didn't care what her size was. If she had flour on her cheek. If she could hit a home run or fuck like a porn star. I wanted to give that to her.

"She deserves more than me."

"I think you're enough, Thatcher Manning," Sarah said. "You're a good man who deserves everything. Don't hold yourself back. It sounds like she has too."

I nodded, thinking of how she'd pushed me away. To protect herself. Her family was a disaster, and she didn't want love because she had horrible examples and it was safer to not to. I steered clear of it because

I'd had such good examples that I knew how amazing it could be. And how devastating when it disappeared.

Like now. With Astrid somewhere else, with her hurting, I wanted to fix it. To take the pain away. For her to give it to me to help. To hand over those reins just as she had in her parents' kitchen.

And that might mean I had to hand over the reins to her right back.

"I gotta go," I said.

Sarah stepped back, nodded.

I fled, knowing exactly what I was going to do.

 STRID

MAYBE I WAS AN IDIOT. Maybe I was going to look back on this moment and cringe. Maybe I was stupid showing up at Thatcher's house in the softball outfit I'd had on all day with my face all blotchy and my eyes swollen. Glancing in the van's rearview mirror, I cringed and wished I hadn't.

But Thatcher knew the worst about me. Knew the very alive skeletons in my closet. Would he still be interested in me after meeting my parents and Amy? God, was he even at the ranch? I'd *left* him in Cutthoat. Was he hitchhiking his way home?

"Shut up, brain," I muttered, slowing as I approached the archway to the Manning Ranch. Small rocks on the dirt road crunched beneath the wheels. I'd never been out this way before, but it was beautiful. The sun was working its way lower in the sky and the prairie was lit in golds and vibrant green. In the distance, I could see the house.

Thatcher's house.

I was doing this. Aunt Jean and Mary had given me a pep talk after I'd blurted out that I was in love with Thatcher. I needed to apologize. To tell him how I felt. That I didn't want anything fake between us. That everything was real.

Some of it, too real.

If I turned around now, Aunt Jean was going to kill me. Mary'd probably quit and that would be bad.

I turned down the driveway, clutching the wheel.

"It's not fake. It's not fake," I repeated as I pulled up in front of the house.

Before I could climb the steps to the porch, the front door opened and a little girl ran out, a small puppy running after her.

She was around five, had blonde hair that was long and damp and she was wearing green pajamas. While she made it down the steps just fine, the puppy tumbled down the last one, popped up with his tongue hanging out and caught up to the little girl.

"You bought Uncle Thatch and you're here for him!"

She hopped up and down in front of me as I looked down at her.

"Um... yes."

"I knew it!"

"Claire," a voice called. I looked to the open doorway and Huck Manning appeared. He gave me a smile. "Sorry about that. She's excited that you're here. You must be Astrid."

Nodding, I said, "Yes. Is Thatcher here?"

"Claire, give her some room."

I looked down at her and stroked her corn silk hair. "You're Claire?"

She nodded.

"I'm Astrid. Who's your friend?" The dog was wiggling and jumping around Claire trying to get her attention.

"Sandy. She's my new dog!"

They were a wiggly duo with the same hair color. Sandy was sweet as could be and clearly loved Claire.

"You are a very lucky girl to have her."

"Thatcher's not here," Huck said, coming down to join us, picking up the puppy and patting her head.

I wilted. My shoulders drooped and I looked down at the ground hoping I didn't start crying again. "Please say he's not hitchhiking back from Cutthroat."

Huck laughed as the dog wiggled and he put her down. Immediately, she tugged at one of his boot laces. "No, he got back. But he's in town."

I lifted my head, looked at Thatcher's brother. They were of a similar size, but they didn't look all that alike. Huck was blond, like Claire.

"Oh. Thanks."

I turned toward my van to leave.

"Astrid, he's in town for you."

THATCHER

I DIDN'T KNOW where Astrid lived. I didn't think of that until I hit the edge of town and had to call Alice. Of course she knew. Turned out Astrid lived above her bakery which was off the far end of Main Street. The building was one of the original stores when the town was founded. Two story and brick, it had a charming front. Parking at the curb, I looked up at the second floor. No lights were on.

The shop was closed, and I went around back to search for a separate apartment entrance. There was none and the van wasn't in the spot off the alley.

I had to call Alice again and ask for Miss Turnbuckle's address. I felt like an idiot, but I was on a mission. I wanted Astrid. I wanted to try her strawberry shortcake and show her my barn house. I wanted to take her to dinner. I wanted to climb in her bed after a night at the Lucky Spur when she was waking up to bake for the day.

I didn't know what any of that really meant except I wanted more. I wanted it to be real.

Miss Turnbuckle didn't live in the library after all, but a small house a few blocks from Claire's preschool. It was painted white with black shutters and glossy front door. Window boxes filled with red flowers flanked the entry. It was neat and tidy, just like the owner.

"Hello, Thatcher," Miss Turnbuckle said when she answered the door. "Who's your friend?" she asked, when the puppy in my arms wiggled and wanted to lick the woman. She laughed as she pet him.

"He doesn't have a name yet. I thought Astrid might name him."

Miss Turnbuckle looked up at me with awe. "The dog's for Astrid? Well done, young man."

The one thing Astrid needed was some unconditional love. If she felt she couldn't get it from people, then she'd get it from a dog. Miss Turnbuckle seemed to think so.

Miss Turnbuckle laughed as the puppy kicked out

his leg over and over when she scratched a spot on his side.

"Is Astrid here?" Since the woman was so short, I peeked into her house over her head. I wasn't one to snoop, but I wasn't in the mood for small talk.

"She's at your ranch, dear."

I looked down at her, stared. "At the ranch?"

She nodded but kept her eyes on the puppy. "She went there for you."

How had we missed each other on the road into town? Her van was pretty obvious.

I pulled out my cell, fumbled with it since I was holding the puppy.

"Astrid's here," Huck said first thing.

I was equally relieved and frustrated.

"Don't let her leave. Sit on her if you have to."

I shoved my phone back in my pocket.

"Ma'am, good seeing you."

"Go, dear." She gave me a smile and a pat on the arm.

I nodded, then hopped in my truck and floored it back to the ranch. Good thing I knew the chief of police to get me out of any speeding tickets.

———

ASTRID

. . .

I SAT on the porch steps beside Huck as we watched Claire and her new puppy run around. I wasn't sure who was chasing who. But they were adorable, and it was impossible not to smile, even when I didn't feel like doing so.

My nerves were getting the best of me since Thatcher called Huck. He patiently waited with me for Thatcher to come from town, but I had a feeling it was more of a babysitting job for me than for watching Claire. He didn't say a word, which was even more unnerving.

When Thatcher came down the drive, I popped up. This was what I'd been wanting to do for an hour. To see him. Talk to him. Yet as I wrung my hands, I wasn't sure if this was such a good idea after all. All my doubts came rushing back and every bold and daring part of me wilted away. I was left unnerved and frazzled. Excited and panicked.

Claire ran over to him when he came toward us, hugging his leg. He gave her a few moments of attention but lifted his head to look at me.

Those blue eyes held mine and the corner of his mouth tipped up. He was holding a puppy, just like Sandy, although this one was black.

"Go on," Huck murmured. "He might just surprise you. He surprised the hell out of me."

Huck stood as well, called to Claire. She ran over

and he squatted down to scoop up Sandy. "Bath, brush, books, bed."

She huffed, then shouted, "I want to read the puppy book!" as she darted into the house.

I heard Huck's retreating footsteps and the front door close, but I couldn't look away from Thatcher.

Unlike me, he'd changed since softball this morning. He had on jeans, sturdy work boots and a white t-shirt that hugged his muscles. I was jealous of the cotton. And the squirming puppy in his arms who just licked his chin.

"Hey," he said, voice deep. Like a rasp of velvet, I almost shivered at that one word.

"Hi."

"Thatcher—"

"Sweets—"

We spoke at the same time, which made us relax.

"Here." He pushed the dog into my arms. I took the cute bundle awkwardly at first, then settled him into my arms.

"Um... what am I doing with this guy?"

"He's yours."

I looked down at the gorgeous big ball of love. He looked up at me with dark eyes, cocking his little head to the side. He was a black Labrador Retriever and I guessed he was eight or nine weeks old. The same size as Sandy.

"Mine?"

He crossed his arms over his chest, watched as the dog's tail thumped against my stomach and he nudged my neck with his soft nose.

"One of Maple's pups. Dogs love unconditionally. They're always happy to see you. They don't care what you look like or who you're friends with. They just want to be where you are."

He reached out, scratched behind his ear and the dog turned his head to try to playfully gnaw on his hand.

"Your parents are a nightmare," he continued. "Your sister's a fucking mess. A dog's a hell of a lot better. This one's a sure thing when it comes to love."

I wasn't sure if I should laugh or cry. Thatcher got me a dog. To give me the love that I wasn't getting from my family.

"Thank you," I said, swallowing hard. I'd never thought about having a dog before, but I lived where I worked. He wouldn't have to be alone, although I'd have to read up on the health codes of animals in a bakery.

I leaned down, nuzzled the puppy.

"I'm sorry about leaving you in Cutthroat," I admitted.

He shrugged as if it wasn't a big deal.

"I'm sorry I didn't give you a chance," he added.

My eyes widened. The puppy wiggled and I put him down. He pranced around, tried to eat a tall blade of grass, then flopped down and went to sleep.

"A chance? Between the party, my parents' house, and softball, I'd say you gave it more than a chance."

He grinned, then leaned in and murmured, "I liked your parents' house. Especially the kitchen."

I flushed and looked down at the dog, pushed my glasses up. "I did, too."

"Go out with me," he said.

I whipped my head up, stared at him. "What?"

"Dinner. Movie. A horseback ride. ATVs. Whatever. I want to spend time with you. Alone."

A thrill shot through me. "You do?"

He grinned, although it was almost bashful. "Yeah."

A few seconds of hope quickly faded. I shook my head. "A weekend is one thing, but I can't go out with you knowing you're leaving. I might be nicer than my sister, but I'm not a masochist."

He set his hand on my arm. The heat of it seeped into me. I remembered what that hand could do, and I got wet. I wanted him to touch me. But I wasn't stupid.

"I'm not going to Mexico."

My eyebrows went up and I stared. "You're not—"

He shook his head. "I texted Kent back and told him no. I connected him with Kelly, my bar manager. She's going to go instead." He paused. "I was running away," he admitted. I could tell the words cost him, because he swallowed hard, looked away for a bit.

"When my friend offered, I thought, what the hell? It would be fun. Easy. A beach and warm weather instead of a Montana winter? It wasn't that hard of a sell. Then Sawyer hooked up with Kelsey and Huck got back together with Sarah. They're in it for the long haul. When I look at them, I see the love my parents had for each other. I'm happy for them, but it's scary as fuck."

I knew his parents had died a long time ago, but nothing more than that.

He sighed, wiped a hand down his face.

"So is having parents who hate each other but stay married," I shared. "That's petrifying to watch because what if I find someone and we turn into that? I only know that kind of love, Thatcher, which probably isn't love at all. You saw it this weekend. I don't want that. It hurts too much."

"You pushed me away to protect yourself," he said, his voice soft. He lifted his hand and stroked my hair.

"You pushed me away to protect *yourself*," I added.

"It hurts too much," I said, repeating her words.

I blinked back tears. "We're a disaster."

He laughed.

"Let's be a disaster together," he murmured.

I looked into his eyes. Saw he was serious.

"We like each other. We wouldn't be feeling like shit without each other if we didn't."

I blinked. He was right.

"I like you," I admitted.

"I like you, too."

I nodded. He nodded.

There. Done.

No, not done.

His hand hooked around to my ponytail and tugged it so my head tipped back. He kissed me.

Yes. Fuck, yes. I loved his kisses and this one was no exception.

With his free hand, he banded his arm around my back and picked me up. Walked forward and set me on a step so we were the same height and he kept right on kissing me.

I wrapped my arms around his neck, held on. Pressed myself into him. Let his tongue find mine. Let him devour me.

We kissed. And kissed. And kissed.

The birds chirped in the far-off trees. The wind whipped across the prairie grass. The sun felt warm on my cheek.

And we kept right on kissing.

"I more than like you," Thatcher said when he started kissing along my jaw.

I clawed at his t-shirt, held on. My breasts pressed into his chest and I knew he could feel how hard my nipples were.

"I'm in love with you." I stilled, suddenly panicked at what I said. "Sorry, that slipped out. Your kisses scramble my brain. I'm a mess and I have no idea what you see in me. I'm in my gym shorts from this morning and I know I'm not crazy thin and—"

Thatcher cut off my rambling with a finger to my lips. I lifted my gaze to his.

"You say anymore bad things about yourself you're going to be over my knee on Huck's front steps."

I frowned. His brother's steps?

"Do you think I care, that I want you to be all dolled up and fancy? That the things you seem to hate about yourself are what makes my dick hard? Haven't you figured out by now that I love you the way you are?"

"But—" I began, then cut myself off. "What?"

"I'm in love with you Astrid. I love your glasses. I love your curves." To back up those words, he slid his hands down my sides and cupped my ass. "I love your giving nature, your smiles." His hands came around and cupped my boobs. "And I love these." His thumbs flicked over my hard nipples.

My nipples believed in mutual attraction.

"I don't think I know what love really is," I shared. "It's not like I had good examples."

"I do. I did. Can we please go to my house so I can show you how much I want to try with you?"

I looked over my shoulder. "You don't live here?"

His hands continued to caress me as he spoke. "I grew up in this house but Huck lives here with Claire and Sarah. Alice, too. I converted the old barn." He moved a hand away to point to his left.

"Yes, show me. Yes, don't go to Mexico. Yes, to dinner or ATVs or both. But whatever you do—" I grabbed his hand and put it back on my boob. "Don't stop."

"I don't plan to, sweets. For a very long time."

 STRID

WE LEFT my van where it was and Thatcher drove me, and the black puppy, further down the drive. He parked in front of a barn and led us inside through a door on the side. I set the puppy down and it scampered off to investigate.

"Come on, I'll show you around," he said, taking my hand. I couldn't get over the space. It did look like a barn, with the thick beams that went up the walls and arched to create a vaulted ceiling, but that was as far as it went. It was one huge room, a second story loft over half of it. The side we entered had no windows that kept the exterior look of the original barn, but the back had wall to wall windows on the lower floor and skylights the entire length of the roof.

It was bright, open and there wasn't a cow or farm animal in sight. The kitchen was modern, with stainless steel appliances and a white granite. The walls were a soft gray, and the furniture was masculine, but there was a mix of vintage pieces, perhaps from the main house that had belonged to his parents, with newer items.

"This is amazing," I said, walking in a circle to take it all in.

He squeezed my hand, led me into his living room area. "I'm glad you like it. I hope you'll be here often."

I lifted my gaze from the view to his blue eyes. Studied him to see if his words were true. He was serious and I felt... elation. Completeness. Some emotion which was unfamiliar, but I liked.

The dog nipped at my ankle and I squatted down to pet him. I couldn't believe he'd gotten me a puppy. He was adorable and I could tell now a complete handful. But he'd been right. The little guy loved me and knew nothing about me. He didn't care the day I'd had. Where I came from. Anything.

He just wanted... me.

It seemed so did this slightly mysterious bartender cowboy. He had layers. So many of them that I wanted to learn. And for some reason, he wanted me. He *loved* me.

Thatcher grabbed a handle on the window and lifted. I realized it was actually a huge garage door made of glass. It rolled up so the section of wall was open to a sprawling deck. The dog forgot about me and ran off exploring again.

"Should we worry about him?" I asked, watching as he sniffed, then toppled off the low deck and onto the grass.

Thatcher smiled as he watched. "Nah. At this age, he won't go far. Besides, he'll have to get used to being here, too." He took my hand again. "Come on."

Leading me to a leather couch, he dropped onto it and pulled me to his lap so I straddled him. Shifting, he moved a throw pillow out of the way.

I took off his hat, set it beside us. "You got your things from my parents' house," I commented, remembering he'd been wearing the stupid ballcap when I'd abandoned him.

He nodded, reaching behind me and carefully removing the hair tie so my hair fell down over my back.

"I did. Your stuff's in my truck."

I shrugged, not caring about the few things I'd taken. I'd figured they were a loss, not willing to return to Cutthroat to get a few outfits. "Doesn't matter."

"It does," he replied. His hands ran over me now, his gaze following their path. It was as if he'd finally been given permission to touch me and couldn't stop.

I didn't want him to.

"I'd miss that green bra and panties set," he admitted. "I want to see you in it again."

"Now?"

His gaze lifted to mine. The blue was dark and stormy. Eager. "Now I want you naked."

I wanted that too, so I took off my t-shirt without any reservation or shyness and dropped it to the floor. "The sports bra is going to take a little work. Guard your eyes."

He frowned. "Huh?"

I laughed. "To hold in the girls, it needs to be tight. Protect yourself from flying elbows." I got to work, crossing my arms in front and grabbing the bottom edge at my ribs. Then worked it up. It wasn't easy and when I was really sweaty, sometimes I panicked I'd get stuck.

Thatcher was laughing by the time it was off but went silent when my breasts were exposed. He looked at them reverently and his fingertips brushed over the indentations the tight fit left in my skin.

"This doesn't hurt, does it?"

I shook my head. "No. It keeps me from getting two black eyes."

He frowned, then caught on. Then cupped me. "They're more than a handful. Perfect. Fuck me, I could play with them for hours."

My nipples tightened into hard points and like a

kid with a new toy—or two—he played with intent focus. Mouth and hands. It wasn't hours, but I was writhing and squirming on his lap eager for more. Interested in giving him some of the same attention. Taking hold of his hands, I moved them off me. He looked up, confused.

I gave him a secret smile, then scooted back and dropped to my knees on the floor between his.

"Sweets," he said, catching on to my intention.

I leaned forward and undid his belt buckle, then his zipper. Thatcher helped by lifting his hips and pushing down his jeans and boxers. His dick sprang free, and I gripped the base. Stroked it once.

"Fuck," he growled, his head falling back to lean against the couch. His eyes remained on me. "The sight of you, my dick at your lips, those tits out and nipples red and hard. Fuck me, it's the prettiest sight I've seen."

I felt powerful then, knowing Thatcher was lost to the pleasure he found in me. In us.

I took him into my mouth for the first time, licking the mushroom shaped head, then taking it deep. There was no way I could take all of him, but I gripped the base and stroked him as I sucked.

His hands tangled in my hair, sliding it back then tugging on it so I looked up at him.

"I don't want to come in your mouth. Not this time. And shit, I don't have a condom. Not here."

"Did you bring the bachelorette party favor bag?" I asked.

His eyes flared and pre-cum dripped from the slit. I flicked it off with my tongue.

"I've got plans for you and those toys. I want you walking around my house in nothing but that jeweled butt plug."

I laughed, but realized he was serious. My butt clenched at the idea. No one had ever gone there before. In any way. But with Thatcher, I wasn't embarrassed. I felt... pretty. Sexy.

He grabbed my arms and pulled me up. "Green's my favorite color." His gaze dropped to my nipple, pulled me close to give one a lick. "Maybe pink."

When he turned and dropped me onto my back down the length of the sofa, he tugged off the rest of my clothes. Pushing my legs apart, he cupped my pussy and said, "Definitely pink."

The feel of him, his weight pressing me into the couch, was incredible. I felt feminine. Desired. Especially since the wet tip of his cock slid across my inner thigh.

"I'm on the pill," I stated, sharing how I protected myself.

He looked down at me, studied my face. "Fuck, sweets. Taking you bare is going to be incredible. I've never done it before."

I shook my head. "Me, either."

He kissed me then. Long, deep. Sweet. He shifted over me, filled me as his mouth claimed mine.

I tipped my head back and gasped at the feel of him.

"Fuck, it's too good."

His forehead leaned against mine.

"Shit. I'm not going to last. I'll make it up to you. But your pussy's dripping all over my dick. It's—"

He stopped talking and thrust into me, wild. Hard. And he came.

I felt it in me, felt it seep out and onto my thighs, his couch.

His breathing was ragged and his skin hot.

It took him a few seconds to recover, then he met me with sated blue eyes. He seemed chagrined that he hadn't lasted. I felt exhilarated, toppling a guy like Thatcher, making him so hot that he came with barely any control.

"Just wait, sweets. That was just to take the edge off. Don't worry, I'll take care of my girl."

I raised my hand, stroked his sweaty cheek. "I know."

"Ladies come first, but today, fuck, you're too much for me. You make me bust a nut like a fifteen-year-old with a girlie magazine." He gazed lowered to my breasts. "Fuck, yeah."

He was still hard inside me. I wasn't even sure that was possible, until now. He took a total of maybe thirty seconds to recover and then he thrust in again. Lowered his head, sucked a nipple into his mouth.

"Your turn," he growled against my skin. "You'll come three times for every time I do."

I stroked his ginger hair. "Three?" I stared up at the ceiling, a little worried. I'd never come three times in a row in my life.

He lifted his head long enough to grin and give me a wink. "Three. Ready for number one?"

Was I?

Was I ready for whatever Thatcher gave me? Whatever we'd be, whatever we'd do together?

Because he was right there with me as he fucked me into orgasm number one. When he flipped me so I knelt facing the back of the couch and took me from behind—with the jeweled plug in my ass—for number two. When he handcuffed me to one of the posts of his bed for orgasm number three.

"Thatcher," I finally moaned, completely wrung out and sprawled naked on his tangled bed sheets.

My glasses had disappeared downstairs. The puppy was sleeping on Maple's dog bed in the corner. Thatcher was coming from his bathroom with a damp cloth. Wearing only his smile.

"Sweets," he said, sitting on the edge of the bed and wiping me between my legs. "What is it?"

I squirmed at the intimacy and the touch on my sensitive pussy. "Are you going to let me go?"

He looked me over, the way my arms trapped over my head thrust my breasts up. Shook his head.

"Good," I replied. "I want you to keep me."

He shifted and loomed over me. Kissed me gently. "Good. Let's keep each other. Do whatever this is our way."

I blinked back tears and smiled. Spread my knees inviting him in. Inviting him home.

"Our way."

———

Did you know Kit Lancaster (the cool event planner) and her hot detective boyfriend, Nix Knight have a book of their own? Nix (along with the barely mentioned Donovan) decide Kit's going to be their's in my steamy, second-chance romance: **Mountain Darkness**. Read it and the entire Wild Mountain Men series now!

We want Kit Lancaster. We've wanted her for years. Both of us. Me and Donovan. It might not be normal for two guys to claim a woman together, but we live in Cutthroat, Montana and we'll do what we want.

And what we want to do is Kit.

What could get in the way? Oh yeah, a little thing called

murder. And since I'm the lead detective and Donovan's the prosecutor, it might not be the smartest thing to bed the prime suspect.

As if that would stop us.

Get Mountain Darkness now!

BONUS CONTENT

Guess what? I've got some bonus content for you! Sign up for my mailing list. There will be special bonus content for some of my books, just for my subscribers. Signing up will let you hear about my next release as soon as it is out, too (and you get a free book...wow!)

As always...thanks for loving my books and the wild ride!

Vanessa

JOIN THE WAGON TRAIN!

If you're on Facebook, please join my closed group, the Wagon Train! Don't miss out on the giveaways and hot cowboys!

https://www.facebook.com/groups/vanessavalewagontrain/

GET A FREE BOOK!

Join my mailing list to be the first to know of new releases, free books, special prices and other author giveaways.

http://freeromanceread.com

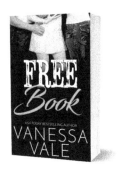

ALSO BY VANESSA VALE

For the most up-to-date listing of my books:

vanessavalebooks.com

All Vanessa Vale titles are available at Apple, Google, Kobo, Barnes & Noble, Amazon and other retailers worldwide.

ABOUT VANESSA VALE

Vanessa Vale is the *USA Today* bestselling author of sexy romance novels, including her popular Bridge-water historical series and hot contemporary romances. With over one million books sold, Vanessa writes about unapologetic bad boys who don't just fall in love, they fall hard. Her books are available world-wide in multiple languages in e-book, print, audio and even as an online game. When she's not writing, Vanessa savors the insanity of raising two boys and figuring out how many meals she can make with a pressure cooker. While she's not as skilled at social media as her kids, she loves to interact with readers.

CPSIA information can be obtained
at www.ICGtesting.com
Printed in the USA
BVHW091633230621
610215BV00008B/1630